THE
SIX DIRECTIONS
OF SPACE

THE
SIX DIRECTIONS
OF SPACE

ALASTAIR REYNOLDS

SUBTERRANEAN PRESS • 2008

Second Printing

ISBN
978-1-59606-184-2

Subterranean Press
PO Box 190106
Burton, MI 48519

www.subterraneanpress.com

W E HAD BEEN RIDING for two hours when I tugged sharply on the reins to bring my pony to a halt. Tenger, my escort, rode on for a few paces before glancing back irritatedly. He muttered something in annoyance—a phrase that contained the words "stupid" and "dyke"—before steering his horse back alongside mine.

"Another sight-seeing stop?" he asked, as the two mismatched animals chewed their bits, flared their nostrils, and flicked their heads up in mutual impatience.

I said nothing, damned if I was going to give him the pleasure of an excuse. I only wanted to take in the view: the deeply-shadowed valley below, the rising hills beyond (curving ever upwards, like a tidal wave formed from rock and soil and grass), and the little patch of light down in the darkness, the square formation of the still-moving caravan.

"If you really want to make that appointment..." Tenger continued.

"Shut up."

Tenger sniffed, dug into a leather flap on his belt, and popped something into his mouth.

"On your own head be it, Yellow Dog. It certainly won't be my neck on the line, keeping the old man waiting."

I held both reins in one hand so that I could cup the other against my ear. I turned the side of my head in the direction of the caravan and closed my eyes. After a few moments, I convinced myself that I could hear it. It was a sound almost on the edge of audibility, but which would become thunderous, calamitous, world-destroying, as they drew nearer. The sound of thousands of riders, hundreds of wheeled tents, dozens of monstrous siege engines. A sound very much like the end of the world itself, it must have seemed, when the caravan approached.

"We can go now," I told Tenger.

He dug his spurs in, almost drawing blood, his horse pounding away so quickly that it kicked dirt into my eyes. Goyo snorted and gave chase. We raced down into the valley, sending skylarks and snipe barrelling into the air.

⋐⋑

"Just going by the rules, Yellow Dog," the guard said, apologising for making me show him my passport. We were standing on the wheeled platform of the imperial *ger*. The guard wore a knee length blue sash-tied coat, long black hair cascading from the dome of his helmet. "We're on high alert as it is. Three plausible threats in the last week."

"Usual nut-jobs?" I said, casting a wary glance at Tenger, who was attending to Goyo with a bad-tempered expression. I had beaten him to the caravan and he did not like that.

"Two Islamist sects, one bunch of Nestorians," the guard answered. "Not that I'm saying that the old man has anything to fear from you, of course, but we have to follow protocol."

"I understand fully."

"Frankly, we were beginning to wonder if you were ever coming back." He looked at me solicitously. "Some of us were beginning to wonder if you'd been disavowed."

I smiled. "Disavowed? I don't think so."

"Just saying, we're all assuming you've got something suitably juicy, after all this time."

I reached up to tie back my hair. "Juicy's not exactly the word I'd use. But it's definitely something *he* has to hear about."

The guard touched a finger to the pearl on his collar.

"Better go inside, in that case."

I did as I was invited.

My audience with the khan was neither as private nor as lengthy as I might have wished, but, in all other respects, it was a success. One of his wives was there, as well as Minister Chiledu, the national security adviser, and the khan was notoriously busy during this ceremonial restaging of the war caravan. I thought, not for the first time, of how old he looked: much older than the young man who had been elected to this office seven years earlier, brimming with plans and promises. Now he was greying and tired, worn down by disappointing polls and the pressures of managing an empire that was beginning to fray at the edges. The caravan was supposed to be an antidote to all that. In this, the nine hundred and ninety ninth year since the death of the Founder (we would celebrate this birthday, but no one knows when it happened), a special effort had been made to create the largest caravan in decades, with almost every local system commander in attendance.

As I stepped off the *ger* to collect Goyo and begin my mission, I felt something perilously close to elation. The data I had presented to the khan—the troubling signs I had detected concerning the functioning and security of the Infrastructure— had been taken seriously. The khan could have waved aside my concerns as an issue for his successor, but—to his credit, I think—he had not. I had been given license and funds to gather more information, even if that meant voyaging to the Kuchlug Special Administrative Volume and operating under the nose of Qilian, one of the men who had been making life difficult for the khan these last few years.

And yet my mood of elation was short lived.

I had no sooner set my feet on the ground than I spied Tenger. He was bullying Goyo, jerking hard on his bridle, kicking a boot against his hocks. He was so preoccupied with his business that he did not see me approaching from behind his back. I took hold of a good, thick clump of his hair and snapped his head back as far it would go. He released the bridle, staggering back under the pressure I was applying.

I whispered in his ear. "No one hurts my horse, you ignorant piece of shit."

Then I spun him around, the hair tearing out in my fist, and kneed him hard in the groin, so that he coughed out a groan of pain and nausea and bent double, like a man about to vomit.

⊂⊃

Some say that it is Heaven's Mandate that we should have the stars, just as it was the will of Heaven that our armies should bring the squabbling lands of Greater Mongolia under one system of governance, a polity so civilised that a woman could ride naked from the western shores of Europe to the eastern edge of China without once being molested. I say that it is simply the case that we—call us Mongols, call us humans, it scarcely matters now—have always made the best of what we are given.

Take the nexus in Gansu system, for instance. It was a medium-sized moon that had been hollowed out nearly all the way to its middle, leaving a shell barely a hundred *li* thick, with a small round kernel buttressed to the shell by ninety nine golden spokes. Local traffic entered and departed the nexus via apertures at the northern and southern poles. Not that there was much local traffic to speak of: Gansu, with its miserly red sun—only just large enough to sustain fusion—and handful of desolate, volatile-poor, and radiation-lashed rocky worlds, was neither a financial nor military hub, nor a place that figured prominently in tourist itineraries. As was often the case, it was something of a puzzle why the wormlike *khorkoi* had built the nexus in such a miserable location to begin with.

Unpromising material, but in the five hundred years since we first reopened a portal into the Infrastructure, we had made a glittering bauble out of it. Five major trunk routes converged on Gansu, including a high-capacity branch of the Kherlen Corridor, the busiest path in the entire network. In addition, the moon offered portals to a dozen secondary routes, four of which had been rated stable enough to allow passage by juggernaut-class ships. Most of those secondary routes led to stellar population centres of some economic importance, including the Kiriltuk, Tatatunga, and Chilagun administrative volumes, each of which encompassed more than fifty settled systems and around a thousand habitable worlds. Even the routes which led to nowhere of particular importance were well-travelled by prospectors and adventurers, hoping to find *khorkoi* relics, or, that fever dream of all chancers, an unmapped nexus.

We did not know the function of the ninety nine spokes, or of the core they buttressed. No matter; the core made a useful foundation, a place upon which to build. From the vantage point of the rising shuttle, it was a scribble of luminous neon, packed tight as a migraine. I could not distinguish the lights of individual buildings, only the larger glowing demarcations of the precincts between city-sized districts. Pressurised horseways a whole *li* wide were thin, snaking scratches. The human presence had even begun to climb up the golden spokes, pushing tendrils of light out to the moon's inner surface. Commercial slogans spelled themselves out in letters ten *li* high. *On Founder's Day, drink only Temujin Brand Airag. Sorkan-Shira rental ponies have low mileage, excellent stamina, and good temperament. Treat your favorite wife: buy her only Zarnuk Silks. During hunting season, safeguard your assets with New Far Samarkand Mutual Insurance. Think you're a real man? Then you should be drinking Death Worm Airag: the one with a sting at both ends!*

I had spent only one night in Gansu, arranging a eunuch and waiting for the smaller ship that would carry us the rest of the way to Kuchlug. Now Goyo, the eunuch, and I were being conveyed to the *Burkhan Khaldun*, a vessel that was even smaller than the *Black Heart Mountain* that had brought me to Gansu. The *BK* was only one *li* from end to end, less than a quarter of that across the bow. The hull was a multicoloured quilt of patch repairs, with many scratches, craters, and scorches yet to be attended to. The lateral stabilisation vanes had the slightly buckled look of something that had been badly bent and then hammered back into shape, while the yaw-dampeners appeared to have originated from a completely different ship, fixed on with silvery fillets of recent welding work. A whole line of windows had been plated over.

As old as the *BK* might have been, it had taken more than just age and neglect to bring her to that state. The Parvan Tract was a notoriously rough passage, quickly taking its toll on even a new ship. If the Kherlen Corridor was a wide, stately river which could almost be navigated blindfold, then the Tract was a series of narrow rapids whose treacherous properties varied from trip to trip, requiring not just expert input from the crew, but passengers with the constitution to tolerate a heavy crossing.

Once I had checked into my rooms and satisfied myself that Goyo was being taken care of, I made my way back to the passenger area. I bought a glass of Temujin *airag* and made my way to the forward viewing platform, with its wide sweep of curved window—scratched and scuffed in places, worryingly starred in others—and leaned hard against the protective railing. The last shuttle had already detached, and the *BK* was accelerating towards the portal, its great human-made doors irising open at the last possible moment, so that the interior of Gansu was protected from the Parvan Tract's unpredictable energy surges. Even though the Infrastructure shaft stretched impossibly far into the distance, my mind kept insisting that we were about to punch through the thin skin of the moon.

The ship surged forward, the sluggish artificial gravity generators struggling to maintain the local vertical. We passed through the door, into the superluminal machinery of the Infrastructure. The tunnel walls were many *li* away, but they felt closer—as they raced by at increasing speed, velocity traced by the luminous squiggly patterns that had been inscribed on the wall for inscrutable reasons by the *khorkoi* builders, I had the impression that the shaft was constricting, tightening down on our fragile little ship. Yet nothing seemed to disconcert or even arouse the interest of my fellow passengers. In ones and twos, they drifted away from the gallery, leaving me alone with my eunuch, observing from a discreet distance. I drank the *airag* very slowly, looking down the racing shaft, wondering if it would be my fortune to see a phantom with my own eyes. Phantoms, after all, were what had brought me here.

Now all I had to do was poison the eunuch.

☾☽

The eunuch answered to "eunuch," but his real name (I learned after a certain amount of probing) was Tisza. He had not been surgically castrated; there was an implant somewhere in his forearm dispensing the necessary cocktail of androgen-blockers, suppressing his libido and lending him a mildly androgynous appearance. Other implants, similar to those employed by government operatives, had given him heightened reflexes, spatial coordination, and enhanced night vision. He was adept with weapons and unarmed combat, as (I had no cause to doubt) were all Batu eunuchs. I had no need of his protection, of course, but appearances were paramount. I was posing as a woman of means, a well-heeled tourist. No women in my circumstances would ever have travelled without the accompaniment of a man such as Tisza.

He served my purpose in another way. We shared the same rooms, with the eunuch sleeping in a small, doorless annex connected to mine. Because I might (conceivably) be drugged or poisoned, Tisza always ate the same meals as me, served at the same time and brought to my cabin by one of the *BK*'s white uniformed stewards.

"What if you get poisoned and die on me?" I asked, innocently, when we were sitting opposite together across my table.

He tapped a pudgy finger against his belly. "It would take a lot to kill me, Miss Bocheng. My constitution has been tailored to process many toxins in common circulation among would-be assassins and miscreants. I will become ill much sooner than you would, but what would kill you would merely make me unwell, and not so unwell that I could not discharge my duties."

"I hope you're right about that."

He patted his chin with napkin. "It is no occasion for pride. I am what I am because of the chemical intervention and surgery of the Batu Escort Agency. It would be equally pointless to understate my abilities."

Later, feigning nervousness, I told him that I had heard a noise from his annex.

"It is nothing, I assure you. No one could have entered these rooms without our knowing it."

"It sounded like someone breathing."

He smiled tolerantly. "There are many foreign sounds on a ship like this. Noises carry a great distance through the ducts and conduits of the air-circulation system."

"Couldn't someone have crawled through those same conduits?"

He rose from the table without a note of complaint. "It is unlikely, but I shall investigate."

As soon as he had vanished through the door into his annex, I produced a vial from my pocket and tipped its sugary contents onto the remains of his meal. I heard him examining things, pulling open cupboard doors and sliding drawers. By the time he returned, with a reassuring expression on his face, the toxin crystals had melted invisibly into his food and the vial was snug in my pocket.

"Whatever you heard, there's no one in there."

"Are you sure?"

"Completely. But I'm willing to look again, if it would put your mind at ease."

I looked abashed. "I'm just being silly."

"Not at all. You must not be afraid to bring things to my attention. It is what you have hired me for."

"Tuck in," I said, nodding at his meal. "Before it gets cold."

⟲⟳

Tisza was moaning and sweating on the bed, deep in fever, as Mister Tayang appraised him warily. "Did he tell you he could detect poisons? They don't all come with that option."

"He can. Isn't that the point?"

"It could just be a bug he's picked up. On the other hand, he may have been hit by something intended for you that his system wasn't designed to filter out."

"A poison?"

"It's a possibility, Miss Bocheng."

Tayang was a steward; a young man with a pleasant face and a highly professional manner. I had seen him around earlier, but—as was the case with all the crew—he had steadfastly refused to engage in any conversation not related to my immediate needs. I had counted on this, and contrived the poisoning of the eunuch to give me heightened access to one or more of the crew. It need not have been Tayang, but my instincts told me that he would serve excellently.

"Then why isn't it affecting me?" I asked.

"I don't wish to alarm you, but it could be that it's going to in a very short while. We need to get both of you into the sick bay. Under observation, we should be able to stabilise the eunuch and insure you come to no harm."

This was the outcome I had been hoping for, but some indignation was called for. "If you think I'm going to spend the rest of this trip in some stinking sick bay, after I've paid for this cabin…"

Tayang raised a calming hand. "It won't be for long. A day or two, just to be on the safe side. Then you can enjoy the rest of the trip in comfort."

Another pair of stewards was summoned to help shift the hapless Tisza, while I made my way to the sick bay on foot. "Actually," I said, "now that you mention it…I do feel a little peculiar."

Tayang looked at me sympathetically. "Don't worry, Miss Bocheng. We'll have you right as rain in no time."

The sick bay was larger and better equipped than I had been expecting, almost as if it belonged in a different ship entirely.

THE SIX DIRECTIONS OF SPACE

I was relieved to see that no one else was using it. Tayang helped me onto a reclined couch while the other stewards pulled a screen around the stricken eunuch.

"How do you feel now?" Tayang asked, fastening a black cuff around my forearm.

"Still a bit funny."

For the next few minutes, Tayang—who had clearly been given basic medical training—studied the readouts on a handheld display he had pulled from a recess in the wall.

"Well, it doesn't *look*..." he began.

"I should have listened to my friends," I said, shaking my head. "They told me not to come here."

He tapped buttons set into the side of the display. "Your friends warned you that you might end up getting poisoned?"

"Not exactly, no. But they said it wasn't a good idea travelling on the *Burkhan Khaldun*, down the Parvan Tract. They were right, weren't they?"

"That would depend. So far, I can't see any sign that you've ingested anything poisonous. Of course, it could be something that the analyser isn't equipped to detect..."

"And the eunuch?"

"Just a moment," Tayang said, leaving the display suspended in the air. He walked over to the other bed and pulled aside the curtain. I heard a murmured exchange before he returned, with a bit less of a spring in his step. "Well, there's no doubt that something pretty heavy's hit *his* system. Could be a deliberate toxin, could be something nasty that just happened to get into him. We're not far out of Gansu; he could have contracted something there that's only just show-ing up."

"He's been poisoned, Mister Tayang. My bodyguard. Doesn't that strike you as a slightly ominous development?"

"I still say it could be something natural. We'll know soon enough. In the meantime, I wouldn't necessarily jump to the conclusion that you're in immediate peril."

"I'm concerned, Mister Tayang."

"Well, don't be. You're in excellent hands." He leaned over to plump my pillow. "Get under the blanket if you feel shivery. Is there anything you'd like me to fetch from your room?"

"No, thank you."

"In which case, I'll leave you be. I'll keep the analyser attached just in case it flags anything. The other stewards are still here; if you need anything, just call."

"I will."

He was on the verge of leaving—I had no doubt that he was a busy man—when something caused him to narrow his eyes. "So if it wasn't about being poisoned, Miss Bocheng, why exactly was it that your friends didn't want you taking this ship?"

"Oh, that." I shook my head. "It's silly. I don't know why I mentioned it all. It's not as if I believe any of that nonsense."

"Any of *what* nonsense, exactly?"

"You know, about the phantoms. About how the Parvan Tract is haunted. I told them I was above all that, but they still kept going on about it. They said that if I took this ship, I might never come back. Of course, that only made me even more determined."

"Good for you."

"I told them I was a rationalist, not someone who believes in ghosts and goblins." I shifted on the couch, giving him a sympathetic look. "I expect that you're fed up with hearing about all that, especially as you actually work here. I mean, if anyone would have been likely to see something, it would be *you*, wouldn't it, or one of the other crew?"

"That would make sense," he said.

"Well, the fact that you obviously *haven't*...there can't be anything to it, can there?" I crossed my arms and smiled triumphantly. "Wait until I tell my friends how silly they've been."

"Perhaps..." he began, and then fell silent.

⊕⊖

I knew that I had him then; that it would be only a matter of time before Tayang felt compelled to show me evidence. My instincts proved correct, for within a day of my discharge from the sick bay (the eunuch was still under observation, but making satisfactory progress), the steward contrived an excuse to visit my quarters. He had a clean towel draped over his arm, as if he had come to replace the one in my bathroom.

"I brought you a fresh one. I think the cleaning section missed this corridor this morning."

"They didn't, but I appreciate the gesture all the same."

He lingered, as if he had something to get off his chest but was struggling to find the right words.

"Mister Tayang?" I pressed.

"What we were talking about before..."

"Yes?" I enquired mildly.

"Well, you're wrong." He said it nicely enough, but the defiance in his words was clear. "The phantoms exist. I may not have seen anything with my own eyes, but I've seen data that's just as convincing."

"I doubt it."

"I can show you easily enough." He must have been intending to say those words from the moment he had decided to come to my cabin, yet now that he had spoken them, his regret was immediate.

"Really?"

"I shouldn't have..."

"Tell me," I said forcefully. "Whatever this is, I want to see it."

"It means your friends were right, and you were wrong."

"Then I need to know that."

Tayang gave me a warning look. "It'll change the way you think. At the moment, you have the luxury of not believing in the phantoms. I know that there's something out there that we don't understand, something that doesn't belong. Are you sure you want that burden?"

"If you can handle it, I think I can. What do I have to do?"

"I need to show you something. But I can't do it now. Later, during the night shift, it'll be quieter."

"I'll be ready," I said, nodding eagerly.

⋐⋑

Close to midnight, Tayang came for me. Remembering to keep in character for someone half convinced she was the target of an assassin, I did not open up immediately.

"Yes?"

"It's me, Tayang."

I cracked open the door. "I'm ready."

He looked me up and down. "Take off those clothes, please."

"I'm sorry?"

He glanced away, blushing. "What I mean is, wear as much or as little as you would wear for bed." I noticed that he had a jacket draped over his arm, as if he was ready to put it around my shoulders. "Should we meet someone, and should questions be asked, you will explain that I found you sleepwalking, and that I'm taking you back to your cabin via the most discreet route I can think of, so you don't embarrass yourself in front of any other passengers."

"I see. You've given this some thought, haven't you?"

"You aren't the first skeptical passenger, Miss Bocheng."

I closed the door and disrobed, then put on thin silk trousers and an equally thin silk blouse, the one scarlet and the other electric yellow, with a design of small blue wolves. I untied my hair and messed it to suggest someone only recently roused from the bed.

Outside, as was customary during the night shift of the *BK*'s operations, the corridor lights were dimmed to a sleepy amber. The bars, restaurants, and gaming rooms were closed. The public lounges were deserted and silent, save for the scurrying mouselike cleaning robots that always emerged after the people had gone away. Tayang chose his route well, for we did not bump into any other passengers or crew.

"This is the library," he said, when we had arrived in a small, red-lit room, set with shelves, screens, and movable chairs. "No one uses it much—it's not exactly a high priority for most of our passengers. They'd rather drink away the voyage with Temujin *airag*."

"Are we allowed here?"

"Well, technically there'd be nothing to stop you visiting this room during normal ship hours. But during normal ship hours, I wouldn't be able to show you what I'm about to." He was trying to be nonchalant about the whole adventure, but his nervousness was like a boy on a dare. "But don't worry, we won't get into trouble."

"How is a library going to change my mind about the phantoms?"

"Let me show you." He ushered me to one of the terminals, swinging out a pair of hinged stools for us to sit on. I sat to the left of him, while Tayang flipped open a dust cover to expose a keyboard. He began to tap at the keys, causing changes to the hooded data display situated at eye-level. "As it happens, these consoles are connected to the *Burkhan*

Khaldun's own computers. You just have to know the right commands."

"Won't this show up?"

He shook his head. "I'm not doing anything that will come to anyone's attention. Besides, I'm perfectly entitled to access this data. The only thing wrong is you being with me, and if anyone comes down here, we'll have time to prepare for them, to make it look as if I caught you sleepwalking." He fell silent for a minute or so, tapping through options, obviously navigating his way through to the information stored in the computer's memory bank. "I just hope the company spooks haven't got to it already," he murmured. "Every now and then, someone from Blue Heaven comes aboard and wipes large chunks of the *BK*'s memory. They say they're just doing routine archiving, clearing space for more data, but no one believes that. Look's like we're in time, though. I didn't see any spooks nosing around when we were in Gansu: they'll probably come aboard next time we're back." He glanced over his shoulder. "I'll show it to you once. Then we go. All right?"

"Whatever you say, Mister Tayang."

"The *BK* has cameras, pointed into the direction of flight. They detect changes in the tunnel geometry and feed that data to the servo-motors driving the stabilising vanes and yaw dampers, so that they can make adjustments to smooth out the turbulence. They're also there as an emergency measure in case we encounter another ship coming the other way, one that isn't on schedule or hasn't got an active transponder. The cameras give us just enough warning to swerve the BK to one side, to give passing clearance. It's bumpy for the passengers when that happens, but a lot better than a head-on collision at tunnel speeds."

"I take it the cameras saw something," I said.

Tayang nodded. "This was a couple of trips ago, about half way between Gansu and Kuchlug. They only got eight clear frames.

Whatever it was was moving fast, much quicker than one of our ships. The fourth, fifth, and sixth frames are the sharpest."

"Show me."

He tapped keys. A picture sprang onto the display, all fuzzy green hues, overlaid with date stamps and other information. It took a moment before I was sure what I was looking at. There was some kind of pale green smudge filling half the frame, a random-looking shape like the blindspot one sees after looking at the sun for too long, and beyond that, a suggestion of the curving squiggles of the tunnel's *khorkoi* patterning, reaching away to infinity.

I pressed a finger against the smudge. "That's the phantom?"

"This is frame three. It becomes clearer on the next one." He advanced to the next image and I saw what he meant. The smudge had enlarged, but also become sharper, with details beginning to emerge. Edges and surfaces, a hint of organised structure, even if the overall shape was still elusive.

"Next frame," Tayang mouthed.

Now there could be no doubt that the phantom was some kind of ship, even if it conformed to the pattern of no vessel I had ever seen. It was sleek and organic looking, more like a darting squid than the clunky lines of the *BK*.

He advanced to the next frame, but—while the image did not become substantially clearer—the angle changed, so that the three-dimensional structure of the phantom became more apparent. At the same time, hints of patterning had begun to emerge: darker green symbols on the side of the hull, or fuselage, or body, of whatever the thing was.

"That's about as good as it gets," Tayang said.

"I'm impressed."

"You see these arm-like appendages?" he asked, pointing to part of the image. "I'm guessing, of course, but I can't help wondering if they don't serve the same function as our stabilisation vanes, only in a more elegant fashion."

"I think you could be right."

"One thing I'm sure of, though. *We* didn't build that ship. I'm no expert, Miss Bocheng, but I know what counts as cutting-edge ship design, and that thing is way beyond it."

"I don't think anyone would argue with that."

"It wasn't built by the government, or some mysterious splinter group of Islamist separatists. In fact, I don't think it was built by humans at all. We're looking at alien technology, and they're using our Infrastructure system as if they own it. More than that: every now and then you hear about entire ships and message packets going missing. They're not just trespassing in our network, they're stealing from it as well."

"I can see Blue Heaven would rather this didn't get out."

Tayang closed the display. "I'm sorry, but that's all I can show you. It's enough, though, isn't it?"

"More than enough," I said.

Of course, I had my doubts. Tayang could have easily faked those images, or been the unwitting victim of some-one else's fakery. But I did not think that was the case. I had been looking at genuine data, not something cooked up to scare the tourists.

I was just beginning to plot my next move—how I would get a copy of the data, and smuggle it back to NHK while I continued with my investigations in Kuchlug space—when I became aware of a presence behind me. Tayang must have sensed it too, for he turned around as I did. Standing in the doorway to the library was one of the other stewards, an older man whose name I had yet to learn. I noticed that the sleeves of his uniform were too short for him.

Wordlessly, he raised a hand. In it glinted the smooth alloy form of a small, precise weapon: the kind often carried by government spies such as myself. He shot me; I had a moment to stare at the barb embedded in my thigh, and then I passed out.

⊂⊃

I came around in my cabin, gripped by a vile nausea, a headache like a slowly closing iron vice, and no conception of how much time had passed since Tayang and I had been disturbed in the library. Getting out of bed—I had been placed on top of the sheets—I searched the adjoining annex for the eunuch, before I remembered that he was still in the sick-bay. I tried my door and found that it had been locked from the outside; there was no way for me to leave my room.

Understand, I did not accept my imprisonment lightly, but understand also that all my attempts at escape proved futile. I could not even squeeze through the conduit I had mentioned to the eunuch: such methods succeed in adventure stories, but not in real life.

Of course, it was desired that I be kept alive. The man who had shot me could have administered a fatal dose simply by twisting a dial in the grip of his weapon. He had chosen not to, and it was no accident that food and water appeared in the room's serving hatch at regular intervals. But as to who had chosen to detain me, I was uninformed.

I could guess, though.

He was the first to see me when the ship docked in Kuchlug space. He came to my room, accompanied by guards. He was as squat and muscled as a wrestler, his bare arms fully as thick as my thighs. He wore a leather jerkin, criss-crossed by thick black belts to which were fastened various ceremonial weapons and symbols of martial authority. A carefully tended moustache, curled down on either side of his mouth, with a tiny but deliberate tuft of hair preserved under his lower lip. A stiff leather helmet, long at the sides and back, covered the rest of his head. The only visible part of his hair was a blunt, wedge-shaped fringe terminating just above his eyebrows, which were at once finely drawn, expressive, and deeply quizzical.

Of course, I knew the face.

"Commander Qilian," I said.

"Yes, I get about." His hands were impressively hairy, scarred and knotted like the roots of a very old tree. He snapped his fingers at the guards. "Have her brought to the debriefing facility on the Qing Shui moon. Bring the pony as well." Then he poked one of those fingers under my chin, lifting it up so that our eyes met. "Give some thought to the particulars of your story, Miss Bocheng. It may make all the difference."

⟵⟶

They took me down to the moon. We landed somewhere and I was carried through dark, rusting corridors to a windowless holding cell. The floor rocked with a slow, sickening motion, as if I was on a ship at sea in a high swell—even though there were no oceans on the Qing Shui moon. They stripped me, took away my belongings, and gave me prison clothing to wear: a simple one-piece affair in orange silk. I pretended to be shocked and disorientated, but I was already summoning my training, recollecting those stratagems I had been taught to withstand prolonged detention and interrogation. As the guards were shutting the door on me, I contrived to slip a finger into the crack between the door and its frame. When the door closed, I yelped in pain and withdrew my hand with the fingertip squashed and red from the pressure.

I sucked it in my mouth until the pain abated.

"Stupid bitch," someone said.

There was a bunk, a spigot in the wall that dribbled tepid, piss-coloured water, and a hole in the floor, with chipped ceramic sides stained an unspeakable brown. Light seeped in through a grille in the door. Neither willing nor able to sleep, I lay on the bunk and shivered. Presently—no more than two or three hours after my arrival—men came to take me down the corridor, to an interrogation room.

It is not necessary to document all that happened; the many weeks that it took for me to permit them to peel back the layers of identity I had wrapped around myself, each time thinking that the victory was theirs.

Suffice to say that most of what they did to me involved electricity and chemicals in varying combinations. They did break two fingers on my left hand, including the one I had trapped in the door, but when they pulled out one of my fingernails, it was from the other hand, not the one I had hurt. They beat me around, broke my teeth, extinguished *Yesugei* brand cigarettes on my skin, but only cut me superficially, to demonstrate that they could and would. Then they had other men come in to sterilise and dress the wounds. Once in a while, a gowned doctor with a Slavic face came to the cell and gave me a thorough, probing medical examination.

It was during one of the doctor's examinations that I elected to reveal myself as a government spy. As the doctor was examining me, I allowed my hair—stiff and greasy with dirt—to fall away from the nape of my neck. I knew instantly that he had taken the bait. I felt his fingers press into the area around the subcutaneous device, feeling for the hard-edged component lodged under the skin.

"What is this?"

"What is what?" I asked, all innocence.

"There's something under your skin."

They took me back to the interrogation room. My hair was shaved and my neck swabbed. The Slavic doctor dithered over the medical tools on the shelves, until he found the bundle he wanted. He brought the instruments onto the table, unrolling the towel so that I could see what lay in store for me. When he was done, the implant was placed on a piece of clean towel in front of me. It was bloodied, with bits of whitish flesh still attached to its feeler-like input probes.

"Looks like government," someone said.

I did not admit to it immediately; that would have made them rightfully suspicious. It was a matter of judging the moment, making my confession appear natural, rather than a scripted event.

In hindsight, I wish that I had arranged my confession sooner.

I was brought to a different room. There was a window in the wall, before which I was encouraged to sit. A clamp was fitted around my eyes so that I could not look away. The doctor dripped some agent into my eyes which had the effect of paralysing the lids, preventing me from blinking. When the lights came on in the room on the other side of the window, I found myself looking at Goyo.

He was upside down, suspended in a sling, rotated on his back in the manner that horses are prepared for veterinary work. The sling was supported from a heavy white framework mounted on trolley wheels. Goyo's legs had been bound together in pairs using thick adhesive material. Even his head and neck had been braced into position using cushioned supports and clamps. A leathery girth strap enclosed his waist, preventing him from thrashing around. His abdominal region, between fore and hind limbs, had been shaved to the skin. A white sheet, not much larger than a towel, had been draped over part of that shaven area. There was a red stain in the middle of the sheet, where it formed a depression.

Goyo's eye, the one that I could see, was white and wild and brimming with fear.

Qilian walked into the room. He was dressed as I remembered him from our encounter on the *BK*, except that his hands and forearms were now gloved. The gloves had a heavy, martial look to them, with curved steel talons on the ends of the fingers. He stopped next to Goyo, one hand resting on the frame, the other stroking my pony's neck, as if he sought to placate him. When he spoke, his voice came through a microphone.

"We think we know who you are, but some corroboration would be welcome. What is your operational codename? To which section are you assigned? Are you one of the Thirteen?"

My mouth had turned dry. I said nothing.

"Very well," Qilian continued, as if he had expected as much. He reached over and whisked the white sheet away from Goyo's abdomen. There was a wound there, a red sucking hole wide enough to plunge a fist through.

"No," I said, trying to break free of the straps that bound me to the chair.

"Before you arrived," Qilian said, "certain surgical preparations were made. A number of ribs have already been removed. They can be put back, of course, but their absence now means that there is an unobstructed path through to your pony's heart."

With his right hand, he reached into the wound. He frowned, concentrating on the task. He delved in slowly, cautiously. Goyo responded by thrashing against his restraints, but it was to more avail than my own efforts. In a short while, Qilian's entire fist was hidden. He pushed deeper, encountering resistance. Now the fist and fully half of his forearm was gone. He adjusted his posture, leaning in so that his chest was braced against Goyo's shoulder. He pushed deeper, until only the top extremity of the glove remained visible.

"I am touching his beating heart now," Qilian said, looking directly at me. "He's a strong one, no doubt about that. A fine pony, from good Mongol stock. But I am stronger, at least when I have my hand on his heart. You don't think I can stop it beating? I assure you I can. Would you like to see?" The expression on his face altered to one of concentrated effort, little veins bulging at the side of his temple. Goyo thrashed with renewed energy. "Yes, he feels it now. He doesn't know what's happening, but a billion years of dumb evolution tells him something's not right. I don't doubt that the pain is excruciating, at least in animal terms. Would you like me to stop?"

The words spilled out, feeling like a genuine confession. "I am Yellow Dog. I am a government operative, one of the Thirteen."

"Yes, we thought you were Yellow Dog. We have the non-official cover list for all of the Thirteen, and we know that Ariunaa Bocheng is a name you've used before, when posing as a journalist." He broke off, took a deep breath, and seemed to redouble his efforts. "But it's good to get it from the horse's mouth, so to speak."

"Stop now."

"Too late. I've already started."

"You said you'd stop," I replied, screaming out the words. "You promised you'd stop!"

"I said nothing of the sort. I said the ribs could be put back. That remains the case."

In an instant, Goyo stopped thrashing. His eye was still open, but all of a sudden there was nothing behind it.

☙❧

Several weeks later—I could not say precisely how many—
Qilian sat opposite me with his big hairy hands clasped in
silent contemplation. The documents on his desk were kept in
place by grisly paperweights: little plinth-mounted bones and
bottled, shrunken things in vinegary solution. There were
swords and ceremonial knives on the wall, framing a familiar
reproduction watercolour showing the landing of the invasion
fleet on Japanese soil.

"You were good," he said eventually. "I'll give you that. My
men genuinely thought they'd hit bottom when they got you to
confess to being the journalist. It was a surprise to all concerned
when that identity turned out to be a cover."

"I'm glad I provided you with some amusement," I said.

"If it hadn't been for that implant, we might never have
known. Your people really should give some thought into making
those things less detectable."

"My people?" I asked. "The last time I checked, we were all
working for the same government."

"I don't doubt that's how it feels in New High Karakorum.
Out here, it's a different story. In case you hadn't realised, this is a
special administrative volume. It's part of the empire, but only in
a very tenuous, politically ambiguous sense. They want what we
can give them—raw materials, cheaply-synthesized chemicals,
mass-produced low-bulk consumer goods—but they don't want
to think too hard about what we have to do to keep that river of
commerce flowing. Laws have to be bent here, because otherwise
there'd *be* no here. Look out the window, Yellow Dog."

Visible through the partially shuttered window of his office,
a good four or five *li* below, was a brutal, wintery landscape of
stained ice, reaching all the way to the horizon. The sky was a
rose pink, shading to midnight blue at the top of the window.
Cutting through it along a diagonal was the twinkling, sickle-like

curve of a planetary ring system. Canyon-deep fissures cracked the surface, leaking feathery quills of yellow-white steam into the thin, poisonous atmosphere of that windswept sky. Here and there, an elbow of splintered rock broke the surface. There were no fixed communities on the moon. Instead, immense spiderlike platforms, mounted on six or eight intricate jointed legs, picked their way across the ever-shifting terrain in awesome slow motion. The platforms varied in size, but at the very least each supported a cluster of squat civic buildings, factories, refineries, and spacecraft handling facilities. Some of the platforms had deployed drilling rigs or cables into the fissures, sucking chemical nourishment from under the icy crust. A number were connected together by long, dangling wires, along which I made out the tiny, suspended forms of cable cars, moving from platform to platform.

"It's very pretty," I said.

"It's a hellhole, frankly. Only three planets in the entire volume are even remotely amenable to terraforming, and not one of those three is on track for completion inside five hundred years. We'll be lucky if any of them are done before the Founder's two thousandth anniversary, let alone the thousandth. Most of the eighty million people under my stewardship live in domes and tunnels, with only a few *alds* of soil or glass between them and a horrible, choking death." He unclasped his hands in order to run a finger across one of his desktop knickknacks. "It's not much of an existence, truth be told. But that doesn't mean we don't have an economy that needs fuelling. We have jobs. We have vacancies for skilled labour. Machines do our drilling, but the machines need to be fixed and programmed by *people*, down at the cutting face. We pay well, for those prepared to work for us."

"And you come down hard on those who displease you."

"Local solutions to local problems, that's our mantra. You wouldn't understand, cosied up in the middle of the empire.

You pushed the dissidents and troublemakers out to the edge and left us to worry about them." He tapped a finger against his desk. "Nestorian Christians, Buddhists, Islamists. It's a thousand years since we crushed them, and they *still* haven't got over it. Barely a week goes by without some regressive, fundamentalist element stirring up trouble, whether it's sabotage of one of our industrial facilities or a terrorist attack against the citizenship. And yet you sit there in New High Karakorum and shake your heads in disgust when we have the temerity to implement even the mildest security measures."

"I wouldn't call mass arrests, show-trials, and public executions "mild"," I said tartly.

"Then try living here."

"I get the impression that's not really an option. Unless you mean living in prison, for the rest of my life, or until NHK sends an extraction team."

Qilian made a pained expression. "Let's be clear. You aren't my enemy. Quite the contrary. You are now an honoured guest of the Kuchlug special administrative volume. I regret what happened earlier, but if you'd admitted your true identity, none of that would have been necessary." He folded his arms behind his neck, leaned back in his chair with a creak of leather. "We've got off on the wrong footing here, you and I. But how are we supposed to feel when the empire sends undercover agents snooping into our territory? And not only that, but agents that persist in asking such puzzling questions?" He looked at me with sudden, sharp intensity, as if my entire future hung on my response to what he was about to say. "Just what *is* it about the phantoms that interests you so much, Yellow Dog?"

"Why should you worry about my interest in a phenomenon that doesn't exist?" I countered.

"Do you believe that, after what you saw on the *Burkhan Khaldun?*"

"I can only report what I saw. It would not be for me to make inferences."

"But still."

"Why are we discussing this, Commander Qilian?"

"Because I'm intrigued. Our perception was that NHK probably knew a lot more about the phenomenon than we did. Your arrival suggests otherwise. They sent you on an intelligence gathering mission, and the thrust of your enquiry indicates that you are at least as much in the dark as we are, if not more so."

"I can't speak for my superiors."

"No, you can't. But it seems unlikely that they'd have risked sending a valued asset into a troublespot like Kuchlug without very good reason. Which, needless to say, is deeply alarming. We thought the core had the matter under control. Clearly, they don't. Which only makes the whole issue of the phantoms even more vexed and troubling."

"What do you know?"

He laughed. "You think I'm going to tell you, just like that?"

"You've as much as admitted that this goes beyond any petty political differences that might exist between NHK and Kuchlug. Let me report back to my superiors. I'll obtain their guarantee that there'll be a two-way traffic in intelligence." I nodded firmly. "Yes, we misjudged this one. I should never have come under deep cover. But we were anxious not to undermine your confidence in us by revealing the depth of our ignorance on the phenomenon. I assure you that in the future everything will be above board and transparent. We can set up a bilateral investigative team, pooling the best experts from here and back home."

"That easy, eh? We just shake hands and put it all behind us? The deception on your part, the torture on ours?"

I shrugged. "You had your methods. I had mine."

Qilian smiled slightly. "There's something you need to know. Two days ago—not long after we dug that thing out of you—we did in fact send a communiqué to NHK. We informed them that one of their agents was now in our safekeeping, that she was being more than helpful in answering our questions, and that we would be happy to return her at the earliest opportunity."

"Go on."

"They told us that there was no such agent. They denied knowledge of either Ariunaa Bocheng or an operative named Yellow Dog. They made no demands for you to be returned, although they did say that if you were handed over, you'd be of "interest" to them. Do you know what this means?" When I refrained from answering—though I knew precisely what it meant—Qilian continued. "You've been disavowed, Yellow Dog. Left out in the cold, like a starving mongrel."

⟲⟳

His men came for me again, several days later. I was taken to a pressurised boarding platform, a spindly structure cantilevered out from the side of the government building. A cable car was waiting, a dull-grey, bulbous-ended cylinder swaying gently against its restraints. The guards pushed me aboard, then slammed the airtight door, before turning a massive wheel to lock it shut. Qilian was already aboard the car, sitting in a dimpled leather chair with one leg crossed over the other. He wore huge fur-lined boots equipped with vicious spurs.

"A little trip, I thought," he said, by way of welcome, indicating the vacant seat opposite his.

The cable car lurched into motion. After reaching the limit of the boarding area, it passed through a long glass airlock and then dropped sickeningly, plunging down so far that it descended under the lowest level of buildings and factory structures perched on the platform. One of the huge, skeletal legs was rising towards us, the foot raised as if it intended to stomp down on the fragile little cable car. Yet just when it seemed we were doomed, the car began to climb again, creaking and swaying. Qilian was looking at something through a pair of tiny binoculars, some piece of equipment—a probe or drillhead, I presumed—being winched up from the surface, into the underside of the platform.

"Is there a point to this journey?" I asked.

He lowered the binoculars and returned them to a leather case on his belt. "Very much so. What I will show you constitutes a kind of test. I would advise you to be on your guard against the obvious."

The cable car slid across the fractured landscape of the moon, traversing dizzyingly wide crevasses, dodging geysers, skimming past tilted rockfaces which seemed on the verge of toppling over at any moment. We rose and descended several times, on each occasion passing over one of the walking platforms. Now and then, there was an interruption while we were switched to a different line, before once more plunging down towards the surface. After more than half an hour of this—just when my stomach was beginning to settle into the rhythm—we came to a definite halt on what was in all respects just another boarding platform, attended by a familiar retinue of guards and technical functionaries. Qilian and I disembarked, with his spurs clicking against the cleated metal flooring. With a company of guards for escort, we walked into the interior of the platform's largest building. The entire place had an oily ambience, rumbling with the vibration of distant drilling processes.

"It's a cover," Qilian said, as if he had read my thoughts. "We keep the machines turning, but this is the one platform that doesn't have a useful production yield. It's a study facility instead."

"For studying what?"

"Whatever we manage to recover, basically."

Deep in the bowels of the platform, at a level which must have meant they were only just above the underside, was a huge holding tank which—so Qilian informed me—was designed to contain the unrefined liquid slurry that would ordinarily have been pumped up from under the ice. In this platform, the tank had been drained and equipped with power and lighting. The entire space had been partitioned into about a dozen ceilingless rooms, each of which appeared to contain a collection of garbage, arranged within the cells of a printed grid laid out on the floor. Some of the cells held sizable clusters of junk, others were empty. Benches arranged around the edges of the cells were piled with bits of twinkly rubbish, along with an impressive array of analysis tools and recording devices.

It looked as if it should have been a literal hive of activity, but the entire place was deserted.

"You want to tell me what I'm looking at here?"

Qilian indicated a ladder. "Go down and take a look for yourself. Examine anything that takes your fancy. Use any tools you feel like. Look in the notebooks and data files. Rummage. Break stuff. You won't be punished if you do."

"This is phantom technology, isn't it? You've recovered pieces of alien ships." I said this in a kind of awed whisper, as if I hardly dared believe it myself.

"Draw whatever conclusion you see fit. I shall be intensely interested in what you have to say."

I started down the ladder. I had known from the moment I saw the relics that I would be unable to resist. "How long have I got? Before I'm judged to have failed this test, or whatever it is."

"Take your time," he said, smiling. "But don't take *too* much."

There seemed little point agonising over which room to start with, assuming I had the time to examine more than one. The one I chose had the usual arrangement of grid, junk, and equipment benches. Lights burned from a rack suspended overhead. I stepped into the grid, striding over blank squares until I arrived at a promising little clump of mangled parts, some of them glittery, some of them charred to near-blackness. Gingerly, I picked up one of the bits. It was a curving section of metallic foil, ragged along one edge, much lighter and stiffer than I felt it had any right to be. I tested the edge against a finger and drew a bead of blood. No markings or detail of any kind. I placed it back down on the grid and examined another item. Heavier this time, solid in my hands, like a piece of good carved wood. Flowing, scroll-like green patterning on one convex surface: a suggestion of script, or a fragmented part of some script, in a language I did not recognise. I returned it to the grid and picked up a jagged, bifurcated thing like a very unwieldy sword or spearhead, formed in some metallic red material that appeared mirror-smooth and untarnished. In my hands, the thing had an unsettling buzzing quality, as if there was still something going on inside it. I picked up another object: a dented blue-green box, embossed with dense geometric patterns, cross-woven into one another in a manner that made my head hurt. The lid of the box opened to reveal six egglike white ovals, packed into spongy black material. There were six distinct spiral symbols painted onto the ovals, in another language that I did not recognise.

I perused more objects in the grid, then moved to the benches, where more items were laid out for inspection.

I moved into one of the adjoining rooms. There was something different about the degree of organisation this time. The grid was the same, but the objects in it had been sorted into rough groupings. In one corner cell was a pile of spiky, metallic red pieces that obviously had something in common with the sword-like object I had examined in another room. In the other lay a cluster of dense, curved pieces with fragmented green patterning on each. Each occupied cell held a similar collection of vaguely related objects.

I examined another room, but soon felt that I had seen enough to form a ready opinion. The various categories of relic clearly had little in common. If they had all originated from the phantoms—either wrecked or damaged or attacked as they passed through the Infrastructure—then there was only one conclusion to be drawn. There was more than one type of phantom, which, in turn, meant there was more than one kind of alien.

We were not just dealing with one form of intruder. Judging by the number of filled cells, there were dozens—many dozens—of different alien technologies at play.

I felt the hairs on the back of my neck bristle. Our probes and instruments had swept the galaxy clean and still we had found no hint of anyone else out there. But these rooms said otherwise. Somehow or other, we had managed to miss the evidence of numerous other galaxy-faring civilisations, all of which were at least as technologically advanced as the Mongol Expansion.

Other empires, somehow coexisting with ours!

I was ready to return to Qilian, but, at the last moment, as I prepared to ascend the ladder, something held me back. It had all been too simple. Anyone with a pair of eyes in their head would have arrived at the same conclusion as I had. Qilian had said it would be a test, and that I must pass it.

It had been too easy so far.

Therefore, I must have missed something.

⋐⋑

When we were back on the cable car, nosing down to the geysering surface, Qilian stroked a finger against his chin and watched me with an intense, snakelike fascination.

"You returned to the rooms."

"Yes."

"Something made you go back, when it looked as if you'd already finished."

"It wouldn't have been in my interests to fail you."

There was a gleam in his eye. "So what was it, Yellow Dog, that made you hesitate?"

"A feeling that I'd missed something. The obvious inference was that the collection implied the presence of more than one intruding culture, but you didn't need me to tell you that."

"No," he acknowledged.

"So there had to be something else. I didn't know what. But when I went back into the second room, something flashed through my mind. I knew I had seen something in there before, even if it had been in a completely different context."

I could not tell if he was pleased or disappointed. "Continue."

"The green markings on some of the relics. They meant nothing to me at first, but I suppose my subconscious must have picked up on something even then. They were fragments of something larger, which I'd seen before."

"Which was?"

"Arabic writing," I told him.

"Many people would be surprised to hear there was such a thing."

"If they knew their history, they'd know that the Arabs had a written language. An elegant one, too. It's just that most people outside of academic departments won't have ever seen it, any more than they know what Japanese or the Roman alphabet looks like."

"But you, on the other hand…"

"In my work for the khanate, I was obliged to compile dossiers on dissident elements within the empire. Some of the Islamist factions still use a form of Arabic for internal communications."

He sniffed through his nostrils, looking at me with his penetrating blue eyes. The cable car creaked and swayed. "It took my analysis experts eight months to recognise that that lettering had a human origin. The test is over; you have passed. But would you care to speculate on the meaning of your observation? Why are we finding Arabic on phantom relics?"

"I don't know."

"But indulge me."

"It can only mean that there's an Islamist faction out there that we don't know about. A group with independent spacefaring capability, the means to use the Infrastructure despite all the access restrictions already in place."

"And the other relics? Where do they fit in?"

"I don't know."

"If I told you that, in addition to items we consider to be of unambiguously alien origin, we'd also found scraps of other vanished or obscure languages—or at least, scripts and symbols connected to them—what would you say?"

I admitted that I had no explanation for how such a thing might be possible. It was one thing to allow the existence of a secret enclave of technologically-advanced Islamists, however improbable that might have been. It was quite another to posit the existence of *many* such enclaves, each preserving some vanished or atrophied branch of human culture.

"Here is what's going to happen." He spoke the words as if there could be no possibility of dissent on my behalf. "As has already been made clear, your old life is over, utterly and finally. But there is still much that you can do to serve the will.

of Heaven. The khanate has only now taken a real interest in the phantoms, whereas we have been alert to the phenomenon for many years. If you care about the security of the empire, you will see the sense in working with Kuchlug."

"You mean, join the team analysing those relics?"

"As a matter of fact, I want you to lead it." He smiled; I could not tell if the idea had just occurred to him, or whether it had always been at the back of his mind. "You've already demonstrated the acuteness of your observations. I have no doubt that you will continue to uncover truths that the existing team has overlooked."

"I can't just…take over, like that."

He looked taken aback. "Why ever not?"

"A few days ago, I was your prisoner," I said. "Not long before that, you were torturing me. They've no reason to suddenly start trusting me, just on your say-so."

"You're wrong about that," he said, fingering one of the knives strapped across his chest. "They'll trust who I tell them to trust, absolutely and unquestioningly."

"Why?" I asked.

"Because that's how we do things around here."

⋐⋑

So it was. I joined Qilian's investigative team, immersing myself in the treasure trove of data and relics his people had pieced together in my absence. There was, understandably, a degree of reluctance to accept my authority. But Qilian dealt with that in the expected manner, and, slowly, those around me came to a pragmatic understanding that it was either work with me or suffer the consequences.

Relics and fragments continued to fall into our hands. Sometimes the ships that intruded into the Infrastructure were damaged, as if the passage into our territory had been a violent one. Often, the subsequent encounter with one of our ships was enough to shake them to pieces, or at the very least dislodge major components. The majority of these shards vanished without trace into the implacable machinery of the Infrastructure. Even if the *khorkoi* apparatus was beginning to fail, it was still more than capable of attending to the garbage left behind by its users. But occasionally, pieces lingered in the system (as if the walls had indigestion?), waiting to be swept up by Qilian's ships, and eventually brought home to this moon.

As often as not, though, it was a trivial matter to classify the consignments, requiring only a glance at their contents. The work became so routine, in fact—and the quantity of consignments so high—that eventually I had no choice but to take a step back from hands on analysis. I assembled six teams and let them get on with it, requiring that they report back to me only when they had something of note: a new empire, or something odd from one of those we already knew about.

That was when the golden egg fell into our hands. It was in the seventh month of my service under Qilian, and I immediately knew that it originated from a culture not yet known to us. Perhaps it was a ship, or part of one. The outer hull was almost entirely covered in a quilt of golden platelets, overlapping in the manner of fish scales. The only parts not covered by the platelets were the dark apertures of sensors and thruster ports, and a small, eye-shaped area on one side of the teardrop that we quickly identified as a door.

Fearing that it might damage the other relics if it exploded under our examinations, I ordered that the analysis of the egg take place in a different part of the mining struc- ture. Soon, though, my concern shifted to the welfare of the egg's occupants. We knew that there were beings inside it, even if we could not be sure if they were human. Scans had illuminated ghostly structures inside the hull: the intestinal complexity of propulsion subsystems, fuel lines, and tanks packed ingeniously tight, the fatty tissue of insulating layers, the bony divisions of armoured partitions, the cartilaginous detailing of furniture and life-support equipment. There were even ranks of couches, with eight crew still reclining in them. Dead or in suspended animation, it was impossible to tell. All we could see was their bones, a suggestion of humanoid skeletons, and there was no movement of those bones to suggest respiration.

We got the door open easily enough. It was somewhat like breaking into a safe, but once we had worked out the underlying mechanism—and the curiously alien logic that underpinned its design—it presented no insurmountable difficulties. Gratifyingly, there was only a mild gust of equalising pressure when the door hinged wide, and none of the sensors arrayed around the egg detected any harmful gases. As far as we could tell, it was filled with an oxygen-nitrogen mix only slightly different from that aboard our own ships.

"What now?" Qilian asked, fingering the patch of hair beneath his lip.

"We'll send machines aboard now," I replied. "Just to be safe, in case there are any booby-traps inside."

He placed a heavy, thick-fingered hand on my shoulder. "What say we skip the machines and just take a look inside ourselves?" His tone was playful. "Not afraid, are we, Yellow Dog?"

"Of course not," I answered.

"There's no need to be. I'll go in first, just in case there *are* surprises."

We walked across the floor, through the cordon of sensors, to the base of the attenuated metal staircase that led to the open door. The robots scuttled out of the way. My staff exchanged concerned glances, aware that we were deviating from a protocol we had spent weeks thrashing out to the last detail. I waved down their qualms.

Inside, as we already knew from the scans, the egg was compartmented into several small chambers, with the crew in the middle section. The rear part contained most of the propulsion and life-support equipment. Up front, in the sharp end, was what appeared to be a kind of pressurised cargo space. The egg still had power, judging by the presence of interior lighting, although the air aboard it was very cold and still. It was exceedingly cramped, requiring me to duck and Qilian to stoop almost double. To pass from one compartment to the next, we had to crawl on our hands and knees through doors that were barely large enough for children. The external door was larger than the others, presumably because it had to admit a crewmember wearing a spacesuit or some other encumbrance.

Qilian was the first to see the occupants. I was only a few seconds behind him, but those seconds stretched to years as I heard his words.

"They are aliens after all, Yellow Dog. Strapped in their seats like little pale monkeys. I can see why we thought they might be human...but they're not, not at all. So much for the theory that every empire must represent a human enclave, no matter how incomprehensible the artefacts or script."

"That was never my theory, sir. But it's good to have it dismissed."

"They have masks on. I can see their faces, but I'd like a better look."

Still on my knees, I said: "Be careful, sir."

"They're dead, Yellow Dog. Stiff and cold as mummies."

By the time I reached Qilian, he had removed one of the intricate masks from the face of his chosen alien. In his hands, it was tiny, like a delicate accessory belonging to a doll. He put it down carefully, placing it on the creature's lap. The alien was dressed in a quilted gold uniform, cross-buckled into the couch. It was the size of an eight year old child, but greatly skinnier in build, its torso and limbs elongated to the point where it resembled a smaller creature that had been stretched. Though its hands were gloved, the layout of the long, dainty-looking digits corresponded exactly to my own: four fingers and an opposed thumb, though each of the digits was uncommonly slender, such that I feared they might snap if we attempted to remove the gloves. Its head—the only part of it not covered by the suit—was delicate and rather beautiful, with huge, dark eyes set in patches of black fur. Its nose and mouth formed one snoutlike feature, suggestive of a dog or cat. It had sleek, intricate ears, running back along the side of its head. Save for the eye patches, and a black nose at the tip of the snout, its skin varied between a pale buff or off-white.

The alien's hands rested on a pair of small control consoles hinged to the sides of the couch; the consoles were flat surfaces embossed with golden ridges and studs, devoid of markings. A second console angled down from the ceiling to form a blank screen at the creature's eye-level. The other seven occupants all had similar amenities. There were no windows, and no controls or readouts in the orthodox sense. The aliens were all alike, with nothing on their uniforms to indicate rank or function. From what little I could see of their faces, the other seven were identical to the one we had unmasked.

I suppose I should have felt awed: here I was, privileged to be one of the first two people in history to set eyes on true aliens. Instead, all I felt was a kind of creeping sadness, and a tawdry, unsettling feeling that I had no business in this place of death.

"I've seen these things before," Qilian said, a note of disbelief in his words.

"These aliens, sir? But this is the first time we've seen them."

"I don't mean that. I mean, isn't there something about them that reminds you of something?"

"Something of what, sir?"

He ignored my question. "I also want this vehicle stripped down to the last bolt, or whatever it is holds it together. If we can hack into its navigation system, find an Infrastructure map, we may be able to work out where they came from, and how the hell we've missed them until now."

I looked at the embossed gold console and wondered what were our chances of hacking into anything, let alone the navigation system.

"And the aliens, sir? What should we do with them?"

"Cut them up. Find out what makes them tick." Almost as an afterthought, he added: "Of course, make sure they're dead first."

⋐⋑

The aliens were not the greatest surprise contained in the egg, but we did not realise that until the autopsy was underway. Qilian and I observed the procedure from a viewing gallery, looking down on the splayed and dissected creature. With great care, bits of it were being removed and placed on sterile metal trays. The interior organs were dry and husk-like, reinforcing the view that the aliens were in a state of mummification: perhaps (we speculated) some kind of suspended animation to be used in emergency situations. But the function and placement of the organs was all too familiar; we could have been watching the autopsy of a monkey and not known the difference. The alien even had a tail, lightly striped in black and white; it had been contained within an extension of the clothing, tucked back into a cavity within the seat.

That the creatures must have been intelligent was not open to dispute, but it was still dismaying to learn how human their brains looked, when they were cut up. Small, certainly, yet with clear division of brain hemispheres, frontal and temporal lobes, and so on. Yet the real shock lay in the blood. It was not necessarily a surprise to find that it had DNA, or even that its DNA appeared to share the same protein coding alphabet as ours. There were (I was led to believe) sound arguments for how that state of affairs might have arisen independently, due to it being the most efficient possible replicating/coding system, given the thermodynamic and combinative rules of carbon-based biochemistry. That was all well and good. But it entirely failed to explain what they found when they compared the alien's chromosomes to ours. More on a whim than anything else, they had tested the alien blood with human-specific probes and found that chromosomes 1 and 3 of the alien were homoeologous to human chromosomes 3, 9, 14, and 21. There were also unexpectedly strong signals in the centromeric regions of the alien chromosomes when probed for human chromosomes 7 and 19. In other words, the alien DNA was not merely similar to ours, it was shockingly, confoundingly, alike.

The only possible explanation was that we were related.

Qilian and I were trying to work out the ramifications of this when news came in from the team examining the pod. Uugan—my deputy—came scuttling into the autopsy viewing room, rubbing sweaty hands together. "We've found something," he said, almost tongue-tied with excitement.

Qilian showed him the hot-off-the-press summary from the genetics analysis. "So have we. Those aliens aren't alien. They came from the same planet we did. I *thought* they looked like lemurs. That's because they *are*."

Uugan had as much trouble dealing with that as we did. I could almost hear the gears meshing in his brain, working through the possibilities. "Aliens must have uplifted lemur stock in the deep past, using genetic engineering to turn them into intelligent, tool-using beings." He raised a finger. "Or, other aliens spread the same genetic material on more than one world. If that were the case, these lemurs need not be from Greater Mongolia after all."

"What news do you have for us?" Qilian asked, smiling slightly at Uugan's wild theorizing.

"Come to the egg, please. It will be easier if I show you."

We hastened after Uugan, both of us refraining from any speculation as to what he might have found. As it happened, I do not think either of us would have guessed correctly.

In the sharp end of the egg, the investigators had uncovered a haul of cargo, much of which had now been removed and laid out on the floor for inspection. I glanced at some of the items as we completed the walk to the pod, recognising bits and pieces from some of the other cultures we already knew about. Here was a branching, sharp-tipped metallic red thing, like an instrument for impaling. Here was a complexly manufactured casket which opened to reveal ranks of nested white eggs, hard as porcelain. Here was a curving section of razor-sharp foil, polished to an impossible lustre. Dozens more relics from dozens of other known empires, and still dozens more that represented empires of which we knew nothing.

"They've been collecting things, just like us," I said.

"Including this," Uugan said, drawing my attention to the object that now stood at the base of the egg.

It was the size and shape of a large urn, golden in construction, surfaced with bas relief detailing, with eight curved green windows set into its upper surface. I peered closer and rested a hand against the urn's throbbing skin. Through the windows burbled a dark liquid. In the dark liquid, something pale floated. I made out the knobbed ridge of a spine, a backbone pressing through flawless skin. It was a person, a human, a man judging by his musculature, curled into foetal position. I could only see the back of his head,: bald and waxy, scribed with fine white scars. Ridged cables dangled in the fluid, running towards what I presumed was a breathing apparatus, now hidden.

Qilian looked through one of the other windows. After a lengthy silence, he straightened himself and nodded. "Do you think he was their prisoner?"

"No way to tell, short of thawing him and out and seeing what he has to say on the matter," Uugan said.

"Do what you can," Qilian told Uugan. "I would very, very much like to speak to this gentleman." Then he leaned in closer, as if what he was about to say was meant only for Uugan's ears. "This would be an excellent time not to make a mistake, if you understand my meaning."

⤆⤇

I do not believe that Qilian's words had any effect on Uugan; he was either going to succeed or not, and the difference between the two outcomes depended solely on the nature of the problem, not his degree of application to the task. As it happened, the man was neither dead nor brain dead, and his revival proved childishly simple. Many weeks were spent in preparation before the decisive moment, evaluating all known variables. When the day came, Uugan's intervention was kept to a minimum: he merely opened the preservation vat, extracted the man from his fluid cocoon, and (it must be said, with fastidious care) removed the breathing apparatus. Uugan was standing by with all the tools of emergency medical intervention at his disposal, but no such assistance was required. The man simply convulsed, drew in several gulping breaths, and then settled into a normal respiratory pattern. But he had yet to open his eyes, or signal any awareness in the change of his surroundings. Scans measured brain activity, but at a level indicative of coma rather than consciousness. The same scans also detected a network of microscopic machines in the man's brain and much of his wider nervous system. Though we could not see these implants as clearly as those we had harvested from the lemur, they were clearly derived from a different technology.

Where had he come from? What did he know of the phantoms?

For weeks, it appeared that we would have no direct answer to these questions. There was one thing, one clue, but we almost missed it. Many days after the man's removal from the vat, one of Uugan's technicians was working alone in the laboratory where we kept our new guest. The lights were dimmed and the technician was using an ultraviolet device to sterilise some culture dishes. By chance, the technician noticed something glowing on the side of the man's neck. It turned out to be a kind of tattoo, a sequence of horizontal symbols that was invisible except under ultraviolet stimulation.

I was summoned to examine the discovery. What I found was a word in Arabic, Altair, meaning eagle, and a string of digits, twenty in all, composed of nine numerical symbols, and the tenth, what the pre-Mongol scholars called in their dead language theca or circulus or figura nihili, the round symbol that means, literally, nothing. Our mathematics incorporates no such entity. I have heard it said that there is something in the Mongol psyche that abhors the very concept of absence. Our mathematics cannot have served us badly, for upon its back we have built a five-hundred year-old galactic empire—even if the *khorkoi* gave us the true keys to that kingdom. But I have also heard it said that our system would have been much less cumbersome had we adopted that Arabic symbol for nothing.

No matter; it was what the symbols told me that was important, not what they said about our choice of number system. In optimistic anticipation that he would eventually learn to speak, and that his tongue would turn out to be Arabic, I busied myself with preparations. For a provincial thug, Qilian had a library as comprehensive as anything accessible from NHK. I retrieved primers on Arabic, most of which were tailored for use by security operatives hoping to crack Islamist terror cells, and set about trying to become an interpreter.

But when the man woke—which was weeks later, by which time it felt as if I had been studying those primers for half my life—all my preparations might as well have been for nothing. He was sitting up in bed, monitored by machines and watched by hidden guards, when I came into the room. Aside from the technician who had first noticed his return to consciousness, the man had seen no other human being since his arrival.

I closed the door and walked to his bedside. I sat down next to him, adjusting the blue silk folds of my skirt decorously.

"I am Yellow Dog," I told him in Arabic, speaking the words slowly and carefully. "You are among friends. We want to help you, but we do not know much about you."

He looked at me blankly. After a few seconds I added: "Can you understand me?"

His expression and response told me everything I needed to know. He spoke softly, emitting a string of words that sounded superficially Arabic without making any sense to me at all. By then I had listened to enough recordings to know the difference between Arabic and baby-talk, and all I was hearing was gibberish.

"I'm sorry," I said. "I do not understand you. Perhaps if we started again, slower this time." I touched a hand to my breast. "I am Yellow Dog. Who are you?"

He answered me then, and maybe it was his name, but it could just as easily have been a curt refusal to answer my question. He started looking agitated, glancing around the room as if it was only now that he was paying due regard to his surroundings. He fingered the thin cloth of his blanket and rubbed at the bandage on his arm where a catheter had been inserted. Once more I told him my name and urged him to respond in kind, but whatever he said this time was not the same as his first answer.

"Wait," I said, remembering something, a contingency I had hoped not to have to use. I reached into my satchel and retrieved a printout. I held the filmy paper before me and read slowly from the adhan, the Muslim call to prayer.

My pronounciation must still not have been perfect, because I had to repeat the words three or four times before some flicker of recognition appeared behind his eyes and he began to echo what I was saying. Yet even as he spoke the incantation, there was a puzzlement in his voice, as if he could not quite work out why we should be engaged in this odd parlour game.

"So I was half-right," I said, when he had fallen silent again, waiting for me to say something. "You know something of Islamic culture. But you do not understand anything I say, except when I speak words that have not been permitted to change in fifteen centuries, and even then you only just grasp what I mean to say." I smiled, not in despair, but in rueful acknowledgement that the journey we had to make would be much longer and more arduous than I had imagined. Continuing in Mongol, so that he could hear my tongue, I said: "But at least we have something, my friend, a stone to build on. That's better than nothing, isn't it?"

"Do you understand me now?" he asked, in flawless Mongol.

I was astonished, quite unable to speak. Now that I had grown accustomed to his baldness and pallor, I could better appreciate those aspects of his face that I had been inclined to overlook before. He had delicate features, kind and scholarly. I had never been attracted to men in a sexual sense, and I could not say that I felt any such longing for this man. But I saw the sadness in his eyes, the homesick flicker that told me he was a long way from family and friends (such as I have never known, but can easily imagine), and I knew that I wished to help him.

"You speak our language," I said eventually, as if the fact of it needed stating.

"It is not a difficult one. What is your name? I caught something that sounded like "filthy hound", but that cannot have been correct."

"I was trying to speak Arabic. And failing, obviously. My name is Yellow Dog. It's a code, an operational identifier."

"Therefore not your real name."

"Ariunaa," I said softly. "I use it sometimes. But around here they call me Yellow Dog."

"Muhunnad," he said, touching his sternum.

"Muhunnad," I repeated. Then: "If you understood my name—or thought you understood it—why didn't you answer me until I spoke Mongolian? My Arabic can't be that bad, surely."

"You speak Arabic like someone who has only heard a whisper of a whisper of a whisper. Some of the words are almost recognisable, but they are like glints of a gold in a stream." He offered me a smile, as if it hurt him to have to criticize. "You were doing your best. But the version of Arabic I speak is not the one you think you know."

"How many versions are there?"

"More than you realise, evidently." He paused. "I think I know where I am. We are inside the Mongol Expansion. We were on the same track until 659, by my calendar."

"What other calendar is there?"

"You count from the death of a warrior-deity; we count from the flight of the Prophet from Mecca. The year now is 1604 by the Caliphate's reckoning; 999 by your own, 2226 by the calendar of the United Nations. Really, we are quibbling over mere centuries. The Smiling Ones use a much older dating system, as they must. The…"

I interrupted him. "What are you talking about? You are an emissary from a previously hidden Islamic state, that is all. At some point in the five hundred years of the Mongol Expansion, your people must have escaped central control to establish a secret colony, or network of colonies, on the very edge of the Infrastructure…"

"It is not like that, Ariunaa. Not like that at all." Then he leaned higher on the bed, like a man who had just remembered an urgent errand. "How exactly did I get here? I had not been tasked to gather intelligence on the Mongols, not this time around."

"The lemurs," I answered. "We found you with them."

I watched him shudder, as if the memory of something awful had only just returned. "You mean I was their prisoner, I think." Then he looked at me curiously. "Your questions puzzle me, Ariunaa. Our data on the Mongols was never of the highest quality, but we had always taken it for granted that you understood."

"Understood *what?*"

"The troubling nature of things," he said.

⟨⟩

The cable car pitched down from the boarding platform, ducking beneath the base of the immense walking platform. After a short while, it came to an abrupt halt, swaying slightly. Qilian pulled out his binoculars and focused on a detail under the platform, between the huge, slowly moving machinery of the skeletal support legs.

"There," he said, passing me the binoculars.

I took them with trembling hands. I had been on my way to Muhunnad for one of our fruitless but not unpleasant conversational sessions, when Quilian's men had diverted me to the cable car platform.

"What am I supposed to be looking at?"

"Press the stud on the side."

I did so. Powerful gyroscopes made the binoculars twist in my hands, tracking and zooming in on a specific object, a thing hanging down from the underside like the weight on the end of a plumb line. I recalled now the thing I had seen the first time Qilian had accompanied me in the cable car, the thing that he had been examining with the binoculars. I had thought it was some kind of test probe or drilling gear being winched back into the platform. I saw now that I had been wrong.

I did need to see his face to know that I was looking at Muhunnad. He had been stuffed into a primitive spacesuit, blackened by multiple exposures to scorching heat and corrosive elements. They had him suspended from his feet, with his head nearest the ground. He was being lowered down towards one of those outgassing rifts in the surface of the Qing Shui moon.

"You can't be doing this," I said.

"If there was any other way," Qilian said, in a tone of utter reasonableness. "But clearly there isn't. He's been dragging his heels, giving us nothing. Spoke too soon early on, confided too much in you, and chose to clam up. Obviously, we can't have that." Qilian opened a walnut-veneered cabinet and took out a microphone. He clicked it on and tapped it against his knee before speaking. "Can you hear me, Muhunnad? I hope your view is as spectacular as ours. I am speaking from the cable car that you may be able to see to your right. We are about level with your present position, although you will soon be considerably lower than us."

"No," I said.

Qilian raised a calming hand. He hadn't even bothered to have me tied into the seat. "Do you hear that, Muhunnad? You still have an admirer." Then he said: "Lower the line, please. Take him to half his present elevation."

"Can you see that he's told you everything he knows?" I asked, tossing the binoculars against the floor.

"He's told us as little as he could get away with," Qilian replied, placing a hand over the end of the microphone to muffle his words. "We could go through the usual rigmarole of conventional interrogation, but I think this will prove much more effective."

"We'll learn far more from him alive than dead."

He looked at me pityingly. "You think I don't know that? Of course I'm not going to kill him. But very soon—unless he chooses to talk—he'll be wishing I did."

The winch dropped Muhunnad to within fifteen or twenty *alds* of the surface, just above the point where the outgassing material became opaque.

"I can hear you," a voice said over the cable car's speaker system. "But I have told you everything I intend to. Nothing you can do now will make any difference."

"We'll see, won't we," Qilian said. To me, confidingly, he said: "By now, he will be in extreme discomfort. You are I are fine, but we have the benefit of a functioning life-support system. His suit is damaged. At the moment, his primary concern is extreme cold, but that will not remain the case for very much longer. As he nears the fissure, it is heat that will begin to trouble him."

"You can tell the woman—Ariunaa—that I am sorry it was necessary to withhold information from her," Muhunnad said. "Her kindness was appreciated. I think she is the only one of you with a heart."

"There's no need for me to tell her anything," Qilian replied. "She's listening in. Aren't you, Yellow Dog?" Somewhat to my surprise, he passed me the microphone. "Talk to him. Reason with your favorite prisoner, if you imagine it will help."

"Muhunnad," I said. "Listen to me now. I have no reason to lie to you. Qilian means what he says. He's going to put you through hell until he finds out what you know. I've seen him murder people already, just to get at the truth."

"I appreciate the concern for my welfare," he said, with a sincerity that cut me to the bone.

"Lower him to five *alds*," Qilian said.

⤆⤇

Is it necessary to document all that happened to Muhunnad? I suppose not; the essential thing is that the pain eventually became intolerable and he began to tell Qilian some of the things my master was desirous of knowing.

What we learned was: Muhunnad was a pilot, a man surgically adapted for optimum control of a ship with extreme Infrastructure agility. His implants were part of the interface system by which he flew his vehicle. It turned out that Muhunnad's people had become aware of the breakdown of Infrastructure integrity many decades ago, long before it had come to our attention.

The difference was, rather than pretending that the problem did not exist, or entrusting it to a single agent like myself, they had dedicated almost their entire state apparatus to finding a solution. Think of Qilian's research, multiplied by a thousand. There were countless men and women like Muhunnad, brave angels tasked with mapping the weak spots in the Infrastructure, the points of leakage, and learning something of the other empires beginning to spill into their own. They knew enough about the properties of those weak points; enough to slip through them, gather intelligence, and still return home. The rate of attrition was still high. Muhunnad was a criminal, convicted of a crime that would have been considered petty in our own society, but which normally merited the death penalty in his. In his case, he had been offered the chance to redeem himself, by becoming a pilot.

They knew about us. They had been intercepting our lost message packets for years, and had even found a couple of our ships with living crew. That was how they had learned Mongolian. They also knew about dozens of other empires, including the lemurs.

"They caught me," Muhunnad said. "As they catch any unwary traveller. They are to be feared."

"They look so harmless," Qilian answered.

"They are vicious beyond words. They are a hive society, with little sense of self. The beings you found, the dead ones, would have sacrificed themselves to ensure their cargo returned home intact. It did not mean that they did so out of any consideration for my well-being. But there are worse things than the lemurs out there. There are the beings we call the Smiling Ones. You will meet them sooner or later. They have been in space for millions of years, and their technology is only matched by their loathing for the likes of you and I."

"Tell us about your state," Qilian probed.

"We call it the Shining Caliphate. It is an empire encompassing seven thousand star systems, comprising twenty thousand settled worlds, half of which are of planet class or at least the size of major moons. A third of those worlds are terraformed or on the way to completion."

"You are lying. If an empire of that size already existed, we would have seen signs of it."

"That is because you are not looking in the right place. The Shining Caliphate is *here*, now, all around you. It occupies much the same volume as your own empire. It even has the same homeworld. You call it Greater Mongolia. We call it Earth."

"Lies!"

But I knew Muhunnad was not lying to us. I think it likely that even Qilian knew it too. He was a brutal man, but not a stupid or unimaginative one. But I do not think he could bare to contemplate his place in a universe in which Muhunnad spoke the truth. Qilian was a powerful man, with an empire of his own on the very edge of the one he was meant to serve. If our empire was a map spread across a table, then he controlled more than could be covered by the palm of a hand. Yet if what Muhunnad said was correct, then that map was but one unexceptional page in a vast atlas, each page a dominion in its own right, of which our own was neither the most powerful, nor the most ancient. Set against such immensity, Qilian controlled almost nothing. For a man like him, that realisation would have been intolerable.

But perhaps I am crediting him with too much intelligence, too much imagination, and he was simply unable to grasp what Muhunnad was telling us.

What he *could* grasp, however, was an opportunity.

I was with them when we brought Muhunnad to the room where the couch had been prepared. I had heard of the existence of the couch, but this was my first sight of it. Even knowing its function, I could not help but see it as an instrument of torture. Muhunnad's reaction, to begin struggling against the guards who held him, showed that he saw the couch in similar terms. Behind the guards loomed white coated doctors and technicians, including the Slav who had torn out my implant.

"This isn't to hurt you," Qilian said magnanimously. "It's to help you."

The couch was a skeletal white contraption, encumbered with pads and restraints and delicate hinged accessories that would fold over the occupant once they had been secured in place.

"I do not understand," Muhunnad said, although I think he did.

"We have studied your implants and deduced something of their function," Qilian said. "Not enough to learn everything about them, but enough to let you control one of our ships, instead of the one you were meant to fly."

"It will not work."

"No one is pretending it will be easy. But it is in your interests to do what you can to make it succeed. Help us navigate the Infrastructure—the way you do, finding the weak points and slipping through them—and we will let you return home."

"I do not believe you."

"You have no option but to believe me. If you cannot assist me in this matter, you will have concluded your usefulness to me. Given the trouble I would get into if New High Karakorum learned of your existence, I would have no option but to dispose of you."

"He means it," I said forcefully. "Help us fly the ships, Muhunnad. Whatever happens, it's better than staying here."

He looked at me as if I was the one thing in the universe he was willing to trust. Given all that had happened to him since leaving his people, it did not surprise me in the slightest.

"Plug him in," Qilian told the technicians. "And don't be too tender about it."

⊖⊖

The name of the ship was the *River Volga*. She was half a *li* in length, her frontal stabilisation spines suggesting the curving whiskers of a catfish. She had been a merchant vehicle once; latterly, she had been equipped for scouring the Parvan Tract for phantom relics, and, most recently, she had been hardened and weaponed for an exploratory role. She would carry six of us: Muhunnad, Qilian, Uugan, and two more members of the technical staff—their names were Jura and Batbayar—and myself. Next to her, identical in almost all respects, was the *Mandate of Heaven*. The only significant distinction between the two craft was that Muhunnad would be piloting the *River Volga*, while the *Mandate of Heaven* followed close behind, slaved to follow the same trajectory to within a fraction of an *ald*. The navigation and steering mechanisms of both ships had been upgraded to permit high-agility manoeuvres, including reversals, close-proximity wall skimming, and suboptimal portal transits. It did not bear thinking about the cost of equipping those two ships, or where the funds had been siphoned from, but I supposed the citizens of the Kuchlug special administrative volume would be putting up with hardships for a little while longer.

We spent five days in shakedown tests before entering the Tract, scooting around the system, dodging planets and moons in high-gee swerves. During that time, Muhunnad's integration into the harness was slowly improved, more and more ship systems brought under his direct control, until he reported the utmost confidence in being able to handle the *River Volga* during Infrastructure flight.

"Are you sure?" I asked.

"Truly, Ariunaa. This ship feels as much a part of me as anything I ever flew in the Shining Caliphate."

"But indescribably less sophisticated."

"I would not wish to hurt your feelings. Given your resources, you have not done too badly."

The transit, when it came, was utterly uneventful. The *Mandate of Heaven* reported some minor buffeting, but this was soon negated following a refinement of the control linkage between the two ships. Then we had nothing but to do but wait until Muhunnad detected one of the points of weakening where, with a judicious alteration in our trajectory, we might slip from one version of the Infrastructure to another.

Did I seriously think that Qilian would keep his promise of returning Muhunnad to his own people? Not really, unless my master had hopes of forging some kind of alliance with the Shining Caliphate, to use as leverage against the central authority of New High Karakorum. If that was his intention, I did not think he had much hope of succeeding. The Caliphate would have every reason to despise us, and yet—given the demonstrably higher level of both their technology and intelligence—there was nothing they could possibly want from us except craven submission and cowering remorse for the holocaust we had visited upon their culture, nearly a thousand years earlier.

No; I did not think Muhunnad stood much chance of returning home. Perhaps he knew that as well. But it was better to pretend to believe in Qilian's promises than incur his bored wrath back on the Qing Shui moon. At least this way, Muhunnad could continue to be materially useful to Qilian, and therefore, too valuable to hurt.

The detection of a weakening in the tunnel geometry, Muhunnad explained, was only just possible given the blunt sensibilities of our instruments. The Caliphate kept detailed maps of such things, but no record had survived his capture by the lemurs, and the information was too voluminous to be committed to memory. He recalled that there were four weak points in the section of Infrastructure we called the Parvan Tract, but not their precise locations or detailed properties.

No matter; he had every incentive to succeed. We overshot the first weakening, but the incident gave Muhunnad a chance to refine the manner in which he sifted the sensor data, and he was confident that he would not make the same error twice. Rather than attempt a reversal, it was agreed to push forward until we encountered the next weakening. It happened two days later, half way to the Gansu nexus. This time, Muhunnad started to detect the subtle changes in the properties of the tunnel in time to initiate a hard slow-down, echoed by the *Mandate of Heaven* immediately to our stern.

We had been warned that the passage would be rough; this was an understatement. Fortunately, we were all braced and ready when it came; we had had two minutes warning before the moment arrived. Even then, the ship gave every indication of coming close to break-up; she whinnied like a horse, her structural members singing as if they had been plucked. Several steering vanes broke loose during the swerve, but the *River Volga* had been equipped to withstand losses that would have crippled a normal ship; all that happened was that hull plates swung open and new vanes pushed out to replace the missing ones. Behind us, the *Mandate of Heaven* suffered slightly less damage; Muhunnad had been able to send correctional steering signals to her guidance system, allowing her to follow a less treacherous path.

And then we were back in the tunnel, travelling normally. To all intents and purposes, it was as if nothing had happened. We appeared to be still inside the Parvan Tract.

"We have become phantoms now," Muhunnad informed us. "This is someone else's Infrastructure."

Qilian leaned over the control couch, where our pilot lay in a state of partial paralysis, wired so deeply into the *River Volga*'s nervous system that his own body was but an incidental detail. Around us, the bridge instruments recorded normal conditions of Infrastructure transit.

"Where are we?"

"There's no way of telling, not with these sensors. Not until we emerge."

"In the Gansu nexus?"

"Yes," he replied. "Or whatever *they* call it. There will be risks; you will not have seen many phantoms emerge into your version of the nexus because most such ships will make every effort to slip through another weakening."

"Why?"

He spoke as if the answer should have been obvious. "Because unless they are pilots like me, on specific intelligence-gathering missions, they would rather keep transitioning between versions of the Infrastructure, than emerge into what is likely to be a densely populated interchange. Eventually, they hope to detect the micro-signatures in the tunnel physics that indicate that they have returned home."

"Signatures which we can't read," I said.

"I will attempt to refine my interpretation of the sensor data. Given time, I may be able to improve matters. But that is some way off."

"We'll take our chances with Gansu," Qilian said.

There was, as I understood it, a small but non-negligible possibility that the weakening had shunted us back into our own version of the Tract—we would know if we emerged into the nexus and I saw advertisements for *Sorkan-Shira* rental ponies.

Muhunnad assured us, however, that such an outcome was very unlikely. Once we were elsewhere, we would only get home again by throwing the dice repeatedly, until our own special number came up.

For all that, when we did emerge into the Gansu nexus, my first thought was that Muhunnad had been wrong about those odds. Somehow or other, we had beaten them and dropped back into our own space. As the door opened to admit us back into the spherical volume of the hollowed-out moon, I had the same impression of teeming wealth; of a city packed tight around the central core, of luminous messages rising up the ninety-nine golden spokes, of the airspace thick with jewel-bright ships and gaudily-patterned, mothlike shuttles, the glittering commerce of ten thousand worlds.

And yet, it only took a second glimpse to see that I was wrong.

This was no part of the Mongol Expansion. The ships were wrong; the shuttles were wrong: cruder and clumsier even than our most antiquated ships. The city down below had a haphazard, ramshackle look to it, its structures ugly and square-faced. The message on the spokes were spelled out in the angular letters of that Pre-Mongol language, Latin. I could not tell if they were advertisements, news reports, or political slogans.

We slowed down, coming to a hovering standstill relative to the golden spokes and the building-choked core. The *Mandate of Heaven* had only just cleared the portal entrance, with the door still open behind it. I presumed that some automatic system would not permit it to close with a ship still so close.

Qilian was a model of patience, by his standards. He gave Muhunnad several minutes to digest the information arriving from the *River Volga*'s many sensors.

"Well, pilot?" he asked, when that interval had elapsed. "Do you recognise this place?"

"Yes," Muhunnad said. "I do. And we must leave, now."

"Why so nervous? I've seen those ships. They look even more pathetic and fragile than ours must have seemed to you."

"They are. But there is no such thing as a harmless interstellar culture. These people have only been in space for a couple of hundred years, barely a hundred and fifty since they stumbled on the Infrastructure, but they still have weapons that could hurt us. Worse, they are aggressors."

"Who are they?" I whispered.

"The culture I mentioned to you back on the Qing Shui moon: the ones who are now in their twenty third century. You would call them Christians, I suppose."

"Nestorians?" Qilian asked, narrowing his eyes.

"Another off-shoot of the same cult, if one wishes to split hairs. Not that many of them are believers now. There are even some Islamists among them, although there is little about the Shining Caliphate that they would find familiar."

"Perhaps we can do business with them," Qilian mused.

"I doubt it. They would find you repulsive, and they would loathe you for what you did to them in your history."

It was as if Muhunnad had not spoken at all. When he alluded to such matters, Qilian paid no heed to his words. "Take us closer to the core," he said. "We didn't weld all this armour onto the *Volga* for nothing."

When Muhunnad did not show readiness to comply with Qilian's order, a disciplinary measure was administered through the input sockets of the harness. Muhunnad stiffened against his restraints, then—evidently deciding that death at the hands of the Christians was no worse than torture by Mongols—he began to move us away from the portal.

"I am sorry," I whispered. "I know you only want to do what's best for us."

"I am sorry as well," he said, when Qilian was out of earshot. "Sorry for being so weak, that I do what he asks of me, even when I know it is wrong."

"No one blames you," I replied.

We had crossed five hundred *li* without drawing any visible attention from the other vessels, which continued to move through the sphere as if going about their normal business. We even observed several ships emerge and depart through portals. But then, quite suddenly, it was as if a great shoal of fish had become aware of the presence of two sleek, hungry predators nosing through their midst. All around us, from one minute to the next, the various craft began to dart away, abandoning whatever course or errand they had been on before. Some of them ducked into portals, or lost themselves in the thicket of spokes, while others fled for the cover of the core.

I tensed. Whatever response we were due was surely on its way by now.

As it happened, we did not have long to wait. In contrast to the civilian vessels attempting to get as far away from us as possible, three ships were converging on us. We studied them on high magnification, on one of the display screens in the *River Volga*'s bridge. They were shaped like arrowheads, painted with black and white stripes and the odd markings of the Christians. Their blade-sharp leading edges bristled with what could have been sensors, refuelling probes, or weapons.

From his couch, Muhunnad said: "we are being signalled. I believe I can interpret the transmission. Would you like to see it?"

"Put it on," Qilian said.

We were looking at a woman, wearing a heavy black uniform, shiny like waxed leather. She was pinned back into a heavily padded seat: I did not doubt that I was looking at the pilot of one of the ships racing to intercept us. Much of her face was hidden under a globular black helmet, with a red-tinted visor lowered down over her eyes. On the crown of the helmet was a curious symbol: a little drawing of the Earth, overlaid with lines of latitude and longitude, and flanked by what I took to be a pair of laurel leaves. She was speaking into a microphone, her words coming over the bridge speaker. I wished I had studied more dead languages at the academy. Then again, given my lack of success with Arabic, perhaps I would still not have understood her Latin either.

What was clear was that the woman was not happy; that her tone was becoming ever more strident. At last, she muttered something that, had she been speaking Mongol, might have been some dismissive invitation to go to hell.

"Perhaps we should turn after all," Qilian said, or started to say. But by then, the three ships had loosed their missiles: four apiece, grouping into two packs of six, one for the *Mandate of Heaven* and one for us.

Muhunnad needed no further encouragement. He whipped us around with all haste, pushing the *River Volga*'s thrust to its maximum. Again, the stress of it was enough to set the ship protesting. At the same time, Muhunnad brought our own weapons into use, running those guns out on their magnetic cradles and firing at the missiles as they closed distance between us and the Christians. Given the range and efficacy of our beam weapons, it would not have troubled him to eliminate the three ships. In concentrating on the missiles, not the pursuers, he was doing all that he could not to inflame matters further. As an envoy of Greater Mongolia, I suppose I should have been grateful. But I was already beginning to doubt that the fate of my empire was going to be of much concern for me.

Because we had turned around, the *Mandate of Heaven* was the first to reach the portal. By then, the door had begun to close, but it only took a brief assault from the *Mandate*'s chaser guns to snip a hole in it. Muhunnad had destroyed nine of the twelve missiles by this point, but the remaining three were proving more elusive; in witnessing the deaths of their brethren, they appeared to have grown more cunning. By the time the *Mandate* cleared the portal, the three had arrived within fifteen *li* of the *River Volga*. By switching to a different fire-pattern, Muhunnad succeeded in destroying two of them, but the last one managed to evade him until it had come within five *li*. At that point, bound by the outcome of some ruthless logical decision-making algorithm, the missile opted to detonate rather than risk coming any closer. It must have hoped to inflict fatal damage on us, even at five *li*.

It very nearly did. I recalled what our pilot had said about there being no such thing as a harmless interstellar culture. The blast inflicted severe damage to our rear shielding and drive assembly, knocking off another two stabilisation vanes.

And then we were through, back into the Infrastructure. We had survived our first encounter with another galactic empire.

More were to follow.

⋐⋑

In my mind's eye, I have an image of a solitary tree, bare of leaves, so that its branching structure is laid open for inspection. The point where each branch diverges from a larger limb is a moment of historical crisis, where the course of world events is poised to swerve onto one of two tracks.

Before his death, our founder spoke of having brought a single law to the six directions of space, words that have a deep resonance for all Mongols, as if it was our birthright to command the fundamental fabric of reality itself. They were prescient words, too, for the bringing of unity to Greater Mongolia, let alone the first faltering steps towards the Expansion, had barely begun. Fifty four years after his burial, our fleet conquered the islands of Japan, extending the empire as far east as it was possible to go. But the day after our fleet landed, a terrible storm battered the harbours of those islands, one that would surely have repelled or destroyed our invasion fleet had it still been at sea. At the time, it was considered a great good fortune; a sure sign that Heaven had ordained this invasion by delaying that storm. Yet who is to say what would have become of Japan, had it not fallen under Mongol authority? By the same token, who is to say what would have become of our empire, if its confident expansion had been checked by the loss of that fleet? We might not have taken Vienna and the cities of western europe, and then the great continents on the other side of the ocean.

I thought of Muhunnad's Shining Caliphate. The common view is that the Islamists were monotheistic savages until swept under the tide of the Mongol enlightenment. But I am mindful that history is always written by the victors. We regard our founder as a man of wisdom and learning first and a warrior second, a man who was respectful of literacy, curious about the sciences, and who possessed a keen thirst for philosophical enquiry. Might the conquered have viewed him differently, I wonder? Especially if our empire fell, and we were not there to gilden his name?

No matter; all that need concern us is that solitary tree, that multiplicity of branches, reaching ever upward. After the moment of crisis, the point of bifurcation, there should be no further contact between one branch and the next. In one branch, the Mongols take the world. In another, the Islamists. In another, some obscure sect of Christians. In another, much older branch, none of these empires ever become a gleam in history's eye.

In an even older one, the lemurs are masters of creation, not some hairless monkey.

But what matters is that all these empires eventually find the Infrastructure. In some way that I cannot quite grasp, and perhaps will never truly understand, the *khorkoi* machinery exists across all those branches. Not simply as multiple copies of the same Infrastructure, but as a single entity that in some way permits the reunification of those branches: as if, having grown apart, they begin to knot back together again.

I do not think this is intentional. If it were, the leaky nature of the Infrastructure would have been apparent to us five hundred years ago. It seems more likely to me that it is growing leaky; that some kind of insulation is beginning to wear away. An insulation that prevents history short-circuiting itself, as it were.

But perhaps I am wrong to second-guess the motives of aliens whose minds we will never know. Perhaps all of this is unfolding according to some inscrutable and deliriously protracted scheme of our unwitting wormlike benefactors.

I do not think we will ever know.

⟳⟲

I shall spare you the details of all the encounters that followed, as we slipped from one point of weakness to another, always hoping that the next transition would be the one that brought us back to Mongol space, or at least into an empire we could do business with. By the time of our eighth or ninth transition, I think, Qilian would have been quite overjoyed to find himself a guest of the Shining Caliphate. I think he would have even settled for a humbling return to the Christians: by the time we had scuttled away from empires as strange, or as brazenly hostile, as those of the Fish People or the Thin Men, the Christians had come to seem like very approachable fellows indeed.

But it was not to be. And when we dared to imagine that we had seen the worst that the branching tree of historical possibilities could offer, that we had done well not to stray into the dominion of the lemurs, that Heaven must yet be ordaining our adventure, we had the glorious misfortune to fall into the realm of the Smiling Ones.

They came hard and fast, and did not trifle with negotiation. Their clawlike green ships moved without thrust, cutting through space as if space itself was a kind of fluid they could swim against. Their beam weapons etched glimmering lines of violet across the void, despite the fact that they were being deployed in hard vacuum. They cut into us like scythes. I knew then that they could have killed us in a flash, but that they preferred to wound, to maim, to toy.

The *River Volga* twisted like an animal in agony, and then there was a gap in my thoughts wide enough for a lifetime.

⋐⋑

The first thing that flashed through my mind after I returned to consciousness was frank amazement that we were still alive; that the ship had not burst open like a ripe fruit and spilled us all into vacuum. The second thing was that, given the proximity of the attacking vehicles, our stay of execution was unlikely to be long. I did not need the evidence of readouts to tell me that the *River Volga* had been mortally wounded. The lights were out, artificial gravity had failed, and in place of the normal hiss and chug of her air recirculators, there was an ominous silence, broken only by the occasional creak of some stressed structural member, cooling down after being heated close to boiling point.

"Commander Qilian?" I called, into the echoing darkness.

No immediate answer was forthcoming. But no sooner had I spoken than an emergency system kicked in and supplied dim illumination to the cabin, traced in the wavery lines of fluorescent strips stapled to walls and bulkheads. I could still not hear generators or the other sounds of routine shipboard operation, so I presumed the lights were drawing on stored battery power. Cautiously, I released my restraints and floated free of my chair. I felt vulnerable, but if we were attacked again, it would make no difference whether I was secured or not.

"Yellow Dog," a voice called, from further up the cabin. It was Qilian, sounding groggy but otherwise sound. "I blacked out. How long was I under?"

"Not long, sir. It can't have been more than a minute since they hit us." I started pulling myself towards him, propelling myself with a combination of vigorous air-swimming and the use of the straps and handholds attached to the walls for emergency use. "Are you all right, sir?"

"I think…" Then he grunted, not loudly, but enough to let me know that he was in considerable pain. "Arm's broken. Wasn't quite secure when it happened."

He was floating with his knees tucked high, inspecting the damage to his right arm. In the scarlet backup lighting, little droplets of blood, pulled spherical by surface tension, were pale colourless marbles. He had made light of the injury but it was worse than I had been expecting, a compound fracture of the radius bone, with a sharp white piece glaring out from his skin. The bleeding was abating, but the pain must have been excruciating. And yet Qilian caressed the skin around the wound as if it was no more irritating than a mild rash.

I paddled around until I found the medical kit. I offered to help Qilian apply the splint and dressing, but he waved aside my assistance save for when it came time to cut the bandage. The *River Volga* continued to creek and groan around us, like some awesome monster in the throes of a nightmare.

"Have you see the others?"

"Uugan, Jura, and Batbayar must still be at their stations in the mid-ship section."

"And the pilot?"

I had only glanced at Muhunnad while I searched for the medical kit, but what I had seen had not encouraged me. He had suffered no visible injuries, but it was clear from his extreme immobility, and lack of response as I drifted by him, that all was not well. His eyes were open but apparently unseeing, fixated on a blank piece of wall above the couch.

"I don't know, sir. It may not be good."

"If he's dead, we're not going to be able to cut back into the Infrastructure."

I saw no point in reminding Qilian that, with the ship in its present state, Muhunnad's condition would make no difference. "It could be that he's just knocked out, or that there's a fault with his interface harness," I said, not really believing it myself.

"I don't know what happened to us just before I blacked out. Did you feel the ship twist around the way I did?"

I nodded. "Muhunnad must have lost attitude control."

Qilian finished with his dressing, inspecting the arm with a look of quiet satisfaction. "I am going to check on the others. See what you can do with the pilot, Yellow Dog."

"I'll do my best, sir."

He pushed off with his good arm, steering an expert course through the narrow throat of the bridge connecting door. I wondered what he hoped to do if the technical staff were dead, or injured, or otherwise incapable of assisting the damaged ship. I sensed that Qilian preferred not to look death in the eye until it was almost upon him.

Forcing my mind to the matter at hand, I moved to the reclined couch that held Muhunnad. I positioned myself next to him, anchoring in place with a foothold.

I examined the harness, checking the various connectors and status readouts, and could find no obvious break or weakness in the system. That did not mean that there was not an invisible fault, of course. Equally, if a power surge had happened, it might well have fried his nervous system from the inside out with little sign of external injury. We had built safeguards into the design to prevent that kind of thing, but I had never deceived myself that they were foolproof.

"I'm sorry, Muhunnad," I said quietly. "You did well to bring us this far. No matter what you might think of me, I wanted you to make it back to your own people."

Miraculously, his lips moved. He shaped a word with a mere ghost of breath. "Ariunaa?"

I took hold of his gloved hand, squeezing it as much as the harness allowed. "I'm here. Right by you."

"I cannot see anything," he answered, speaking very slowly. "Before, I could see everything around me, as well as the sensory information reaching me from the ship's cameras. Now I only have the cameras, and I am not certain that I am seeing anything meaningful through them. Sometimes I get flashes, as if *something* is working…but most of the time, it is like looking through fog."

"Are you sure you can't make some sense of the camera data?" I asked. "We only have to pass through the Infrastructure portal."

"That would be like threading the eye of a needle from half way around the world, Ariunaa. Besides, I think we are paralysed. I have tried firing the steering motors, but I have received no confirmation that anything has actually happened. Have you felt the ship move?"

I thought back to all that had happened since the attack. "In the last few minutes? Nothing at all."

"Then it must be presumed that we are truly adrift and that the control linkages have been severed." He paused. "I am sorry; I wish the news was better."

"Then we need help," I said. "Are you sure there's nothing else out there? The last time we saw it, the *Mandate of Heaven* was still in one piece. If she could rendezvous with us, she might be able to carry us all to the portal."

After a moment, he said: "There is something, an object in my vicinity, about one hundred and twenty *li* out, but I only sense it intermittently. I would have mentioned it sooner, but I did not wish to raise your hopes."

Whatever he intended, my hopes were rising now. "Could it be the *Mandate?*"

"It is something like the right size, and in something like the right position."

"We need to find a way to signal it, to get it to come in closer. At the moment, they have no reason to assume any of us are alive."

"If I signal it, then the enemy will also know that some of us are still alive," Muhunnad answered. "I am afraid I do not have enough directional control to establish a tight-beam lock. I am not even certain I can broadcast an omnidirectional transmission."

"Broadcast what?" Qilian asked, drifting into the bridge.

I wheeled around to face him; I had not been expecting him to return so quickly. "Muhunnad says there's a good chance the *Mandate of Heaven* is nearby. Since we don't seem to able to move, she's our only chance of getting out of here."

"Is she intact?"

"No way to tell. There's definitely something out there that matches her signature. Problem is, Muhunnad isn't confident that we can signal her without letting the enemy know we're still around."

"It won't make any difference to the enemy. They'll be coming in to finish us off no matter what we do. Send the signal."

After a moment, Muhunnad said: "It's done. But I do not know if any actual transmission has taken place. The only thing I can do is monitor the *Mandate* and see if she responds. If she has picked up our signal, then we should not have long to wait. A minute, maybe two. If we have seen nothing after that time, I believe we may safely assume the worst."

We waited a minute, easily the longest in my life, then another. After a third, there was still no change in the faint presence Muhunnad was seeing. "I am more certain than ever that it is the *Mandate*," he informed us. "The signature has improved; it matches very well, with no sign of damage. She is holding at one hundred and twenty *li*. But she is not hearing us."

"Then we need another way of signalling her," I said. "Maybe if we ejected some air into space…"

"Too ambiguous," Qilian countered. "Air might vent simply because the ship was breaking up, long after we were all dead. It could easily encourage them to abandon us completely. What do we need this ship for in any case? We may as well eject the lifeboats. The *Mandate of Heaven* can collect them individually."

After a instant of reflection, Muhunnad said: "I think the commander is correct. There is nothing to be gained by staying aboard now. At the very least, the lifeboats will require the enemy to pursue multiple targets."

There were six lifeboats, one for each of us.

"Let's go," Qilian replied.

"I'll see you at the lifeboats," I said. "I have to help Muhunnad out of the harness first."

Qilian looked at me for a moment, some dark calculation working itself out behind his eyes. He nodded once. "Be quick about it, Yellow Dog. But we don't want to lose him. He's still a valued asset."

ⅭↃ

With renewed strength, I hauled the both of us through the echoing labyrinth of the ship, to the section that contained the lifeboats. It was clear that the attack had wrought considerable damage on this part of the ship, buckling wall and floor plates, constricting passageways and jamming bulkhead doors tight into their frames. We had to detour half way to the rear before we found a clear route back to the boats. Yet although we were ready to don suits if necessary, we never encountered any loss of pressure. Sandwiched between layers of the *River Volga*'s outer hull was a kind of foam that was designed to expand and harden upon exposure to vacuum, quickly sealing any leaks before they presented a threat to the crew. From the outside, that bulging and hardening foam would have resembled a mass of swollen dough erupting through cracks in the hull.

There were six lifeboats, accessed through six armoured doorways, each of which was surmounted with a panel engraved both with operating instructions and stern warnings concerning the penalties for improper use. Qilian was floating at the far end, next to the open doorway of the sixth boat. I had to look at him for a long, bewildered moment before I quite realised what I was seeing. I wondered if it was a trick of my eyes, occasioned by the gloomy lighting. But I had made no mistake. Next to Qilian, floating in states of deceptive repose, were the bodies of Jura and Batbayar. A little further away, as if he had been surprised and killed on his own, was Uugan. They had all been stabbed and gashed: knife wounds to the chest and throat, in all three instances. Blood was still oozing out of them.

In his good hand, Qilian held a bloody knife, wet and slick to the hilt.

"I am sorry," he said, as if all that situation needed was a reasonable explanation. "But only one of these six boats is functional."

I stared in numb disbelief. "How can only one be working?"

"The other five are obstructed; they can't leave because there is damage to their launch hatches. This is the only one with a clear shaft all the way to space." Qilian wiped the flat of the blade against his forearm. "Of course, I wish you the best of luck in proving me wrong. But I am afraid I will not be around to witness your efforts."

"You fucking…" I began, before trailing off. I knew if I called him a coward he would simply laugh at me, and I had no intention of giving him even the tiniest of moral victories. "Just go," I said.

He drew himself into the lifeboat. I expected some last word from him, some mocking reproach or grandiloquent burst of self-justifying rhetoric. But there was nothing. The door clunked shut with a gasp of compressed air. There was a moment of silence and stillness and then the boat launched itself away from the ship on a rapid stutter of electromagnetic pulses.

I felt the entire hull budge sideways in recoil. He was gone. For several seconds, all I could do was breathe; I could think of nothing useful or constructive to say to Muhunnad, nothing beyond stating the obvious hopelessness of our predicament.

But instead, Muhunnad said quietly: "We are not going to die."

At first, I did not quite understand his words. "I'm sorry?"

He spoke with greater emphasis this time. "We are going to live, but only if you listen to me very, very carefully. You must return me to the couch with all haste."

I shook my head. "It's no good, Muhunnad. It's all over."

"No, it is not. The *River Volga* is not dead. I only made it seem this way."

I frowned. "I don't understand."

"There isn't time to explain here. Get me back to the bridge, get me connected back to the harness, then I will tell you. But make haste! We really do not have very much time. The enemy are much nearer than you think."

"The enemy?"

"There is no *Mandate of Heaven*. Either she scuttled back to the portal, or she was destroyed during the same attack that damaged us."

"But you said…"

"I lied. Now help me move!"

Not for the first time that day, I did precisely as I was told.

Having already plotted a route around the obstructions, it did not take anywhere near as long to return to the bridge as it had taken to reach the lifeboats. Once there, I buckled him into the couch—he was beginning to retain some limb control, but not enough to help me with the task—and set about reconnecting the harness systems, trusting myself not to make a mistake. My fingers fumbled on the ends of my hands, as if they were a thousand li away.

"Start talking to me, Muhunnad," I said. "Tell me what's going on. Why did you lie about the *Mandate*?"

"Because I knew the effect that lie would have on Qilian. I wished to give him a reason to leave the ship. I had seen the kind of man he was. I knew that he would save himself, even if it meant the rest of dying."

"I still don't understand. What good has it done us? The damage to the ship…" I completed the final connection. Muhunnad stiffened as the harness took hold of his nervous system, but did not appear to be in any obvious discomfort. "Are you all right?" I asked warily.

"This will take a moment. I had to put the ship into a deep shutdown, to convince Qilian. I must bring her back system by system, so as not to risk an overload."

The evidence of his work was already apparent. The bridge lights returned to normal illumination, while those readouts and displays that had remained active were joined by others that had fallen into darkness. I held my breath, expecting the whole ensemble to shut back down again at any moment. But I should have known better than to doubt Muhunnad's ability. The systems remained stable, even as they cycled through start-up and crash recovery routines. The air circulators resumed their dull but reassuring chug.

"I shall dispense with artificial gravity until we are safely underway, if that is satisfactory with you."

"Whatever it takes," I said.

His eyes, still wide open, quivered in their sockets. "I am sweeping local space," he reported. "There was some real damage to the sensors, but nowhere as bad as I made out. I can see Qilian's lifeboat. He made an excellent departure." Then he swallowed. "I can also see the enemy. Three of their ships will shortly be within attack range. I must risk restarting the engines without a proper initialisation test."

"Again, whatever it takes."

"Perhaps you would like to brace yourself. There may be a degree of undamped acceleration."

Muhunnad had been right to warn me, and even then it came harder and sooner than I had been expecting. Although I had managed to secure myself to a handhold, I was nearly wrenched away with the abruptness of our departure. I felt acceleration rising smoothly, until it was suppressed by the dampeners. My arm was sore from the jolt, as if it had been almost pulled from its socket.

"That is all I can do for us now," Muhunnad said. "Running is our only effective strategy, unfortunately. Our weapons would prove totally ineffective against the enemy, even if we could get close enough to fire before they turned their own guns on us. But running will suffice. At least we have the mass of one less lifeboat to consider."

"I still don't quite get what happened. How did you know there'd still be one lifeboat that was still working? From what I saw, we came very close to losing all of them."

"We did," he said, with something like pride in his voice. "But not quite, you see. That was my doing, Ariunaa. Before the instant of the attack, I adjusted the angle of orientation of our hull. I made sure that the energy beam took out five of the six lifeboat launch hatches, and no more. Think of a knife fighter, twisting to allow part of his body to be cut rather than another."

I stared at him in amazement, forgetting the pain in my arm from the sudden onset of acceleration. I recalled what Qilian had said, his puzzlement about the ship twisting at the onset of the attack. "You mean you had all this planned, before they even attacked us?"

"I evaluated strategies for disposing of our mutual friend, while retaining the ship. This seemed the one most likely to succeed."

"I am...impressed."

"Thank you," he said. "Of course, it would have been easier if I had remained in the harness, so that we could move immediately once the pod had departed. But I think Qilian would have grown suspicious if I had not shown every intention of wanting to escape with him."

"You're right. It was the only way to convince him."

"And now there is only one more matter that needs to be brought to your attention. It is still possible to speak to him. It can be arranged with trivial ease: despite what I said earlier, I am perfectly capable of locking on a tight-beam."

"He'll have no idea what's happened, will he? He'll still think he's got away with it. He's expecting to be rescued by the *Mandate of Heaven* at any moment."

"Eventually, the nature of his predicament will become apparent. But by then, he is likely to have come to the attention of the Smiling Ones."

I thought of the few things Muhunnad had told us about our adversaries. "What will they do to him? Shoot him out of the sky?"

"Not if they sense a chance to take him captive with minimal losses on their own side. I would suggest that an unpowered lifeboat would present exactly such an opportunity."

"And then?"

"He will die. But not immediately. Like the Shining Caliphate, and the Mongol Expansion, the Smiling Ones have an insatiable appetite for information. They will have found others of his kind before, just as they have found others of mine. But I am sure Qilian will still provide them with much amusement."

"And then?" I repeated.

"An appetite of another kind will come into play. The Smiling Ones are cold-blooded creatures. Reptiles. They consider the likes of us—the warm, the mammalian—to be a kind of affront. As well they might, I suppose. All those millions of years ago, we ate their eggs."

I absorbed what he said, thinking of Qilian falling to his destiny, unaware for now of the grave mistake he had made. Part of me was inclined to show clemency: not by rescuing him, which would place *us* dangerously close to the enemy, but by firing on him, so that he might be spared an encounter with the Smiling Ones.

But it was not a large part.

"Time to portal, Muhunnad?"

"Six minutes, on our present heading. Do you wish to review my intentions?"

"No," I said, after a moment. "I trust you to do the best possible job. You think we'll make it into the Infrastructure, without falling to pieces?"

"If Allah is willing. But you understand that our chances of returning to home are now very slim, Yellow Dog? Despite my subterfuge, this ship *is* damaged. It will not survive many more transitions."

"Then we'll just have to make the best of wherever we end up," I said.

"It will not feel like home to either of us," he replied, his tone gently warning, as if I needed reminding of that.

"But if there are people out there...I mean, instead of egg-laying monsters, or sweet-looking devils with tails, then it'll be better than nothing, won't it? People are people. If the Infrastructure is truly breaking down, allowing all these timelines to bleed into one another, than we are all going to have get along with each other sooner or later. No matter what we all did to each other in our various histories. We're all going to have to put the past behind us."

"It will not be easy," he acknowledged. "But if two people as unlike as you and I can become friends, then perhaps there is hope. Perhaps we could even become an example to others. We shall have to see, shan't we?"

"We shall have to see," I echoed.

I held Muhunnad's hand as we raced towards the portal, and whatever Heaven had in store for us on the other side.